I0760391

# Planting The House

Richard Blevins

SPUYTEN DUYVIL
*New York City*

This is a work of fiction. Names, characters, places, and incidents either are the product of the author's imagination or are used fictitiously, and any resemblance to actual persons, living or dead, businesses, companies, events, or locales is entirely coincidental.



ISBN 978-1-952419-25-6 pbk | 978-1-952419-27-0 hdc.

Library of Congress Cataloging-in-Publication Data

Names: Blevins, Richard, author.
Title: Planting the house / Richard Blevins.
Description: New York City : Spuyten Duyvil, [2020] |
Identifiers: LCCN 2020026258 | ISBN 9781952419256 (paperback) | ISBN 9781952419270 (hardcover)
Classification: LCC PS3503.L635 P58 2020 | DDC 813/.54--dc23
LC record available at https://lccn.loc.gov/2020026258

*To Kent Johnson*

# Editors' Note

In his final days, Elwin Roe, a career sociologist and author of a monograph on Eric Fromme (1968), came to understand that writing the two books he hoped to live to finish, a novel of the American West (*The Virginian*) simultaneously with a memoir of childhood ("Preacher"), made its own story amounting to an accidental novel. Roe's editors have endeavored to retain the richness of his methodology of alternating in daily writing sessions between the twin piles of growing manuscripts—of one mind here spontaneously overlapping; there blending paragraphs. The resulting art is "not a statue but a mosaic," as Robert Duncan said of the odes of Pindar. In the weeks before President Trump finally acknowledged the pandemic, the virus spread like wildfire, killing Elwin Roe before he finished writing "Preacher." He had lived to be Goethe's age when he gave the world *Faust II*. While the editors have remained faithful to the author's texts, notes, and expressed wishes, the title for the freestanding novel was left to our deliberation, one we borrow from "Breed," a song by Kurt Cobain that Roe loved.

We are grateful to the caregivers at Cleveland Clinic, Cleveland, Ohio. Special thanks go to Kent State University Libraries, Special Collections, where the manuscript of this novel is preserved in Box 27 of the Richard Blevins Papers.

*The Virginian* sections of this novel are reprinted courtesy of Spuyten Duyvil Press. "Preacher" sections are published by permission of the Estate of Elwin Charles Roe. The Tarkovsky epigraph is from his essay collection, translated by Kitty Hunter-Blair (1987).

*Conscience is the anticipation of the fellow who awaits you if and when you come home* —
HANNAH ARENDT, *THE LIFE OF THE MIND.*

*Time is a state: the flame in which there lives the salamander of the human soul* —
ANDREY TARKOVSKY, *SCULPTING IN TIME.*

*Fire on its approach will judge and condemn everything*—
HIPPOLYTUS, *REFUTATION OF ALL HERESIES.*

*if you want a revolution*
*return to your childhood*
*and kick out the bottom*
D.A. LEVY, "TOMBSTONE AS A LONELY CHARM."

ECONOMY FAMILY TYPE
A.H. BOMB SHELTER
Milwaukee's 1st
FAMILY TYPE
A.H. BOMB SHELTER

# 1. Preacher
# "Quo Vadis?"

The old man could not make the short distance to the shelter most of one whole week in February. He measured the backyard snowfall with his yard stick, 27 inches overnight, and then it froze. He told the boy out loud he guessed school was cancelled for those days, Outlaw. Regardless, the ghost boy was not free to sleep all morning or play all afternoon; he could only brood in the corners of cold rooms. At last, the old man trudged through the snow and, exhausted, reached the door to the shelter. His gloved hands removed the crust of snow but he was soon defeated, the trap door frozen solid. So the old man limped his way back through the snow, like a docent to work at some unvisited war memorial, a wind behind him obliterating his tracks. Snow blind inside the house, he had to feel a way to his chair. It felt odd to relight the carbide headlamp and wear the miner's cap inside the house. His pant legs were soaked, his socks were miserably wet and cold, but he was too weary to change clothes. He must have looked funny too because the ghost boy made a show of laughing soundlessly while clapping his hands to the sound of water dripping. The house lost power that night. The rooms grew almost as cold as outdoors. The dead boy inwhistled not making a cloud of breath. Kent Johnson worried that the old man might have died, when his emails went unanswered. The old man dozed off before the lights came to life some hour of an early morning. The fallout shelter was an Arctic station perfectly encased inside a blue block of ice, he dreamed, his radio knocked out of commission by a solar flare. Now the old man will have to work feverishly, two times as hard, to finish the books before dying.

**Early Draft, How the Memoir Begins**

From the street, the house looks abandoned.

The abandoned boy drives him from the house each morning, drives him each morning underground.

Underground the room awaits the old man, out in the neglected yard, where he buries himself in work, the work that teaches him a thing underground has a life of its own, that instead of a life of his own in the writing one thing follows another, the writing that will not leave the boy from his childhood out in the yard, on a hill of coal where the now dead once assembled in a week the rebarbative Sears bungalow.

The prospect of the Sears bungalow spontaneously igniting into flames, never enters the passerby's head.

Passersby head for the front yard to stop long enough for their dogs' shit.

Someone dropped a dirty diaper on the driveway like the morning newspaper...

The old man tried to write about the house but it made neither verse nor prose, neither paragraph nor fragment, like a trailer for an upcoming feature.

**"Epitaphing"**

"A fire was ignited, on May 27, 1962," he typed, "in an abandoned coal mine underneath Centralia, Pennsylvania.

"Having burned now for half a century, it could burn for another 200 years.

"As the fire progresses along rich seams of coal, hot and poisonous gases are vented up into riven basements of homes and businesses, jetting around headstones in the cemetery and new upheavals moving measurably down unnavigable 61 North."

The newspaper clipping came as a kind of revelation, not the one the old man had been expecting for decades—instead, the shame that burned but would not consume him.

"I know how it feels to grow up feeling superior for no good reason, spending childhood…landlocked…in the fictional land…kingdom only white supremacy could…idealize."

He has been faithfully taking his prescribed dose of THC for a month now. The old man's pain seems unaffected; he does notice a fluency in his writing, but not the typing, one hour after he swallows the pill. He pecks out one letter at a time, chipping away at an epitaph.

## 2. The Virginian

Each morning before dawn, in all kinds of weather, the old man takes his second coffee into the backyard where he writes for two hours, in the iron lung-shaped room down beneath the hanging wisteria. He is default survivor of the fallout shelter. Bolted in from the inside, he feels suspended in times of his own choosing—in the act of writing, he forgets to fear he will die before he finishes—he must only think to crank the Kearny air pump once upon entering and again after the first hour, both times with the motion he uses to sharpen a pencil. Thirty years ago, the Cold War bunker was stripped of its original wiring and VW battery. His one innovation is to write by the flame from a miner's headlamp, which he lights and claps on his head before climbing down the ladder into the dark. Water from the top of the miner's four-inch headlamp drips onto the carbide housed in the brass bottom, the chemical reaction releases acetylene gas under pressure through the tip pointing out of the polished tin two-and-a-half-inch reflector like a stamen from a flower, a striker wheel ignites the gas to produce the yellow flame trimmed to one inch up to one-and-a-half inches long. After every use, the miner's headlamp must be disassembled and cleaned. Once he begins writing, the coffee congeals in the cup. The old man does not need to remember the waiting boy, the boy who tries to sit still a little way off in the dark. The old man is the ghost boy's de facto amanuensis: if he runs his hand across his face, a shadow crosses the typed page. (Sometimes, a clumsy projectionist got in the way of his movie or some kid would hurl a paper wad from his seat, and the screen had a live shadow momentarily. Such shadows were the real world intruding by mistake, he has come to think.) Each day, the old man resumes his underground novel about the Trump Age, a verbatim retyping of the 1911 edition of *The Virginian*. Counting the new Author's Preface, he figures the novel, if he lives to finish it, will come in under 700 manuscript pages. *The Virginian* is being published serially online by Kent Johnson at the *Dispatches from the Poetry Wars* blog. The boy is always ready when the first hour passes so the old man can set aside his novel, satisfied today to have added new pages 501 through 511, and pick up where he left off yesterday in "Preacher," a memoir of the old man's childhood in the haunted house—both childhood and house loom over him while he works.

Twenty years ago, following his widowed mother's death in the house, the old man resumed residence and presumed, at his age, the writing of novels. He tried at first to churn out a true tale of the Wild West, but became derailed at the train station. The Emeritus-Associate-Professor-of-Education in the old man fretted that his knowledge of the historical West, of the objects and horses and clothing and drink that constituted 1880s Wyoming, the acoustics of daily life, inadequate elementary knowledge not really understood, echoing crazily down the corridors of history—violently clashing against the code of the West and the laws of language—and into the too small space of his aging ears. He was sure he couldn't survive a month in those towns. Nothing, he felt, is more unbearable than watching *Hamlet* on stage in modern dress. He felt he needed to train himself, and quick, to block the peripheral vision of footnotes—see the page instead of his nose: focus his thought into the beam from his headlamp. He felt, for the first time in his eighty-some years, alone: he had to ring his own number to see if his phone still worked. It took him four years of hard labor to excavate the first book from the sediment of his aged brain, *The Assassination of Thomas Merton*, a short novel about the kind of college town where he'd taught for 43 years. After the book was published to the general applause of water dripping, the old man struggled before the idea for *The Virginian* surfaced. In the end, it was Donald J. Trump, the new Teddy Roosevelt, who made the western novelist: he found permission to compose *The Virginian* now that the language in the White House was Wister-speak; now that the Eternal Flame was fed by the toxic language of another white supremacist's hatred of otherness, for a long time dormant beneath our land like natural gas unfracked. When the old man got the bad news, the country was already *distant stage.*

To start, he tries out a sentence he'd carried outside in his head this morning, "I am a victim of the Wild West." The old man really doesn't see how this sentence could make the beginning of a book, but he types out the rest anyway figuring how things fit as he went. The fallout shelter had been carefully designed so that everything, every single thing from the fold-up bed/seat to the dining table/cabinet, fit. The art of the novel seemed to be to shoe horn in everything in the world but carefully toss out all the wrong words. "I lived to see my country strangled by a White House made in the image of Owen Wister's heroic

West. I have a name for this mass hysteria: it is Wisteria. And I am a victim of the Wild West a hundred years after the West was closed." He never could compose on the computer. For several weeks now, he had been taking notes for his preface by hand in the house at night and then taking them out to the shelter to type up. When he got enough, he would scan the ogham pages at the library and email them to the publisher from one of the free computers. Our elite white author of *The Virginian* is an insider who full well knows but does not acknowledge the fact that one in every four historical cowboys, or up to 9,000 workers in the cattle industry from the Civil War through the Range Wars, was a black man.

MEDICINE BOW IS ABOUT 100 MILES northwest of Cheyenne (Laramie marks the halfway point on the drive), home for the 90th Space Wing, who keep 150 Minuteman III missiles and 50 Peacekeeper missiles at the ready in underground silos. It is the largest and most up-to-date missile unit in the country. If you look for it you will find preserved, hard by the Lincoln Highway and the railroad tracks leading out of town, the Owen Wister Suite inside the Virginian Hotel in Medicine Bow. The three-story building stands apart, detached in its conspicuous whiteness as Crane's blue hotel, not so much rising from the Wyoming plains as having been dropped there out of the big sky. The room, where he never worked or even decamped overnight, features one of Wister's desks from somewhere. The naming of hotel and suite are instances of Owen Wister's haunting of America. Consigning Wister to history means more than we suspect. His novel sold 20,000 copies in its first month of publication 116 years ago, but to many readers today an allegory of Social Darwinism on the western frontier will feel as familiar as a live stream MAGA rally. You see, our 45th president unwittingly mouths the very language the formulaic cowboy hero. Wister is the hand inside the Trump puppet, whose ventriloquist's voice is the tough-guy speech of "rugged individualism" marketed by our president and by the friend of a sitting president. On sale is nothing less than the American heroic myth. How did we as a country arrive at Trump? At a racist-in-chief who impulsively spews Social Darwinisms, his mind innocent of history, ideology, laws, details of policy—a grafter who closets himself with unelected advisors like Stephen Miller who are foremost the terminal Go-Getters of late-stage white supremacy? *The Virginian* maps one path here. Scipio might just as well be warning us about Donald Trump when he counsels the Virginian that "When a man ain't got no ideas of his own, he'd ought to be kind of careful who he borrows 'em from." (Chapter XXIII)

Donald Trump and Owen Wister were born a century apart into lives of eastern wealth and privilege, far removed from the frontier conditions out of which a "self-made" cowpoke might be said to evolve into a "natural aristocrat." The socially finished creator of the cowboy hero had nothing in him of the self-made man. Wister, like his future unpolished counterpart The Donald, was connected: famed actress of the London stage Fanny Kemble, a doting grandmamma, arranged for the young Owen to perform on the piano for Franz List; while at Harvard, he wrote and produced a Hasty Pudding's show; he was Harvard University and Harvard Law; he dedicated his *Virginian* to President Theodore Roosevelt, whose critique had caused Wister to mitigate two violent scenes; he first traveled to Wyoming for a rest cure ordered by the physician novelist S. Weir Mitchell; a great-grandfather had been a delegate from South Carolina to the Constitutional Convention; he was twice a Channing by marriage, descendant from the Transcendentalist William Ellery Channing.

All great historical figures, the historian observed, appear twice: the first time is tragedy, the second is farce. Steve Bannon likened the newly inaugurated Trump to Andy Jackson, so the president hanged Jackson's portrait conspicuously in the Oval Office. But the heady comparison mistakes Jackson's populism for the Teddy Roosevelt variety. Wister's "best man" teaches himself to read Shakespeare and Walter Scott's *Kenilworth*, but his feat is outshone by a semi-literate who hates to read. Donald Trump has authored a new reading of the classic novel, a *Vir-*

*ginian* for the 21st century. Seen through the lens of *The Virginian*, Trump appears as an etiolated Social Darwinist, a puppet fronting a nationalist movement he does not contemplate. Wister's elitist message to the masses is as clear as the photographs of Steve Mnuchin and Louise Lintor posing with uncut sheets of dollar bills.

Once, the pugilist Roosevelt addressed the nation from his Bully Pulpit...

Sunday mornings lately, our bully president Tweets to the faithful from his bed in Palm Beach.

He typed the above an hour ago and reading it now in the house above ground makes him think of something his mother once told him, when he worried about the flower garden hiding the fallout shelter, "If you do somehow plant a bulb upside down, it just takes a little longer to sprout."

The old man has saved a clipping from the Sunday paper to remind himself that "Render to God and Trump" was the original title for *For God and Country: the Christian case for Trump*, a new book by Ralph Reed, founder of Faith and Freedom Coalition. He archived it in the file folder labeled "THE VA: Religion." Day sound filters down to him, purified by the ground; he remains mostly in the dark of surrounding roots and suffixes. The old man recalls how Sunday sermons once welled up in front of him in the spotlit air beyond the church balcony where he sat as a boy inspired, breathing in the word of God.

He is working through his mother's book of Henry James' stories as part of his amateur's study of culture in Owen Wister's era. Just today, he read "The Jolly Corner" for the first time. He judged a passage to be important. "He found all things come back to the question of what he personally might have been, how he might have led his life and 'turned out,' if he had not so, at the outset, given it up. And confessing for the first time to the intensity within him of this absurd speculation—which but proved also, no doubt, the habit of too selfishly thinking—he affirmed the impotence there of any other source of interest, any other native appeal. 'What would it have made of me, what would it have made of me?' I keep for ever wondering, all idiotically; as if I could possibly know! I see what it has made of dozens of others, those I taught at school and those who were my boyhood friends, and it positively aches within me, to the point of exasperation, that it would have made something of me as well. Only I can't make out *what,* and the worry of it, the small rage of curiosity never to be satisfied, brings back what I remember to have felt, once or twice, after judging best, for reasons, to burn some important letter unopened. I've been sorry, I've hated it—I've never known what was in the letter."

The old man bookmarked the passage with another book, holding it a sin to place an open book facedown and break the spine. Henry James sentences flattened him.

The fallout shelter makes a most unstable house.

It gets too hot inside, the air gets bad. He must pack in the most elementary items, light and water, and then they are in constant threat of running low or expiration dates. Nonperishables. Shelf life. Every surface, each object is present for its functionality, unflinchingly beyond the nostalgia of beauty. He has a house without a family history (it only goes back as far as Steuart Pittman). His house does not advertise a permanent address.

It is too artsy for him to imagine the house as a root cellar wherein the living are suspended like so many dormant bulbs. Christian dead awaiting the second coming. Nonperishables. Half-life. If abstraction was the grand effort to update art, modernism retiring the tired law of perspective, then what radical departure is called for by the fallout shelter? Its curving metal walls will not tolerate the art museum's ark, the two of all things, the likeness and its abstract. Frames work like windows, and pictures only slide down resistanceless curving metal walls: and crash. The shelter is not a time capsule. Items to be collected inside the shelter must be carefully selected for utility and size, so salt mines stuffed with stolen Nazi art cannot be the model. Underground, all images of art, nature, family, sports, cities would be unbearable windows into what is forever denied—a missing child on a milk carton. This is what insurance looks like in concrete form. His father the builder paid toward this every month. Supplied this form with the basics every season. Praying he would never use it.

(Heinlein tried to build a literary fallout shelter, during the time when he was actually constructing one at his house, the old man read with interest. "Barbara looked around. It was an L-shaped room; they had entered the end of one arm. Two bunks were on the right-hand wall… The left wall was solid with packed shelves; the passage was hardly wider than the door. The ceiling was low and arched and of corrugated steel. She could see the ends of two more bunks at the bend…The space between the bays was filled by pressure bottles, a water tank, a camp toilet, stores, and a small area where a person might manage a stand-up bath. The air intakes and exhausts, capped off, were there, plus a hand-or-power blower, and scavengers for carbon dioxide and water vapor. This space was reached by an archway between the tiers of bunks."

The survivors in *Farnham's Freehold* emerge blinking from the shelter the father built and try to focus in an Afro-centric world order—the family's black servant is become overseerer! As if, after the late revelations, Dallas Billington's houseboy is installed as deacon.)

Self-quarantined, our every thought a second thought.

His fallout shelter is not the house where generations lived and gave birth and died at home. The blast door in the Flower Garden has no history, only anecdotes. The old man as a boy often hid there on especially hard days, instead of playing with cretin cousins or going to school. One time he did fall asleep in the shelter and get busted for playing hooky when he suddenly resurfaced for suppertime. Even then he knew to make up a story on the spot about the ferocious German shepherd chasing him home from school, so the mother reheated a plate for him when the father had withdrawn for the night.

It still pisses him off.

By the time his mother passed away, the one minister the local Baptist church could attract was a kid of maybe 38 or 40, just starting his own family in a town foreign to him. He had only recently been called from his work at a Big Lots in his native Dover to preach. The rookie preacher had interviewed the old man's 93-year-old mother (at her request) sometime in the weeks before her death; it fell to him to preside at her funeral (she'd planned a gala affair), and he'd been taught at Bob Jones seminary that he needed to pad out his narrative of her life with personal anecdotes to make a eulogy the community would talk about. The old man will never know exactly what she told him (she was mentally lucid till her final day on earth and it wasn't like Marie to put anybody on) but at the funeral, after the preacher slow-walked through a hagiography of this godly Christian woman, things went terribly wrong, so wrong the old man had the god-damnedest time keeping himself from shouting down the holy bastard in front of her open casket. The idiot preacher told the gathered together for some reason that his mother did dearly love to travel (the old man knew she rarely left the county, but took one big trip out to Boulder with her second husband to see her 75-year-old kid sister and suffered every one of the 3,000 miles from back pain aggravated by the epic car ride and vertigo in the motel rooms from Minears disease reactivated by rapid changes in elevation between the mountains and salt flats—she said she especially wanted to see if rocks really can move on their own across the Death Valley Floor, making trails in the sand like the snails of Bruge; and once she rode a Greyhound to Indianapolis to see a childhood friend who later drowned herself, pregnant again, by walking into a pond with stones in her pockets) and how she returned, from every single place she visited, carrying a souvenir rock or at least palming a stone, and this she placed in her flower garden (had the assistant minister looked for himself, he would have seen only mulch there and a raw flint lawn ornament)! The old man's memory of the mother's funeral is quarantined by the outrageous grotesque picture of her on a multi-state rampage, prying loose pieces of landscape from national parks and motel lawns, piling up the stolen loot in the floor of his step-father's Buick—when they make it home and he opens the passenger door for her, a cascade of pilfered rocks and minerals, including a stray shard of petrified wood, pale pink coral, and a meteorite fragment, unloads itself into their driveway. The newly motherless son had to strain to restrain himself from revealing the sham story, but in the end he just folded into his folding chair for the eternity it took the preacher. He regularly fantasizes about stoning the young man the very next June 27—he throws the first stone—but there are no stones here, never were. Mom hated weeding sentimental clutter.

NO LAW COULD STOP HIM!! UNTIL HE CAME FACE TO FACE WITH THE...
J. FRANCIS WHITE, Jr. and JOY HOUCK
KING OF THE BULLWHIP
STARRING "LASH" LaRUE · "FUZZY" St. JOHN
JACK HOLT · TOM NEAL
ANNE GWYNNE
MICHAEL WHALEN · WILLIS HOUCK · MARY LOU WEBB
DENNIS MOORE · JIMMIE MARTIN · CLIFF TAYLOR
Produced and Directed by RON ORMOND · IRA WEBB
Story and Screenplay by JACK LEWIS and IRA WEBB
A WESTERN ADVENTURE PRODUCTION

# 3. Preacher
# "Reel One"

At long last, the lights go down. The epic begins in media res, as it must begin, and every kid in the theater knows well how the story goes. The wheels of our stagecoach whirl backwards to propel us here again.

**"King of the Bullwhip"**

Lash LaRue was Preacher's very favorite.

Today the colored boy is retelling *King of the Bullwhip,* which he'd seen the afternoon before. If he watched a Lash LaRue short in between two features/a cartoon/and a newsreel, he always picks the cowboy serial to retell. Those Sundays after church, the boys from the street met, regardless of weather or season or health, inside the oily tool shed hunched at the rear of four back yards, to listen rapt to the colored boy's recital of what he saw at the Saturday matinee. The boy had just come from the Negro evangelical church, and the boy who is now the old man from the white evangelical church across town, so the Southern Baptist hell-fire and brimstone poured into our ears now poured out of his mouth, all the worn plots in perfect contradiction, the ritual deaths of Hollywood and Holy Bible, and the guys of course ate it up. An old-time tent revival indeed! But always when he stopped speaking—Amen!—the guys roused themselves as if from a trance, and breathing again the boy returned to being 'Tard or Rat Fink or Preacher, returned to being the only Negro they knew and despised.

"OK. You won't believe this one, but I swear, on my grandma's grave, this is what I saw...."

"Aw, jesusfuckinchrist, cut the bushwah, willya Preacher, or we'll take ya out back right now and string ya up for good this time."

"I'm serious, Cliff, I swear. There's finally this new Lash LaRue movie I know we've all been waiting for, the first one in years, and they opened it up BY SHOWING THE END OF THE MOVIE FIRST! The whip fight with the masked mystery criminal mastermind who turns out to be the guy from town I figured all along—."

"Bull. Shit."

"Ok, just let me tell it. You'll love this. The movie, ahem, is called *King of the Bullwhip*!"

"An yer the Prince of Bullsheet. Somebody please shoot me, I'm in pain! Oh, Sissy LaRue!"

"Fuck off, Cliff," he tried a desperate joss to distract Cliff and maybe draw his fire away from the kid. "We wanna hear, if you don't. Pay no attention to this card shark. Go ahead, Preacher."

**"All Westerns Are Contemporaneous"**

The old man who was the boy thinks he intuited this truism as a young boy. Ron Ormond, and before him Ray Taylor, mixed old footage into their new films. The same guard gets shot and topples off the same careening stagecoach; the same hombre gets drilled and dies falling his way down the outside stairs; the locale, including two complete movie towns, a wooden one on a steep one-street hill and the other a stone affair, reached by well-travelled dirt trails winding out of the arroyo in front of fantastically shaped rock formations, is dream-familiar as the Iverson Movie Ranch in Chatsworth, California, and especially its Garden of the Gods and Alabama Hills sections; the same close-up of the maddened faces of wild-eyed horses pulling a stagecoach recklessly—the wheels of the stagecoach hypnotize. All true aficionados of the movie serial are obsessives. Whole landscapes, odd rock formations, trails, towns, and action scenes featuring fast riding that takes too long to make a good film, obsessively revisited as in a recurring dream at once soothingly familiar and disquieting.

Sometimes the Negro boy got mixed up in his retelling, or found he had to add a scene from another film to pad his time with the boys like a savvy evangelist.

**"He Swears, They Take His Breath Away"**

Those close-ups in *King of the Bullwhip* are something new from Ormond, this first film he directed for his new studio. Lash's 20-foot grimace and his 15-foot fist thrown in anger across the big screen ambush his senses. When the despicable El Azote's whip wraps around Lash's neck—you can see the hero's eyes bulge, the sweat on his brow, blood pressure rising dangerously—the masked bastard pulls Lash closer—our hero breaks his hold with a blown-up blow that knocks the dirty rat to the ground. But then LaRue does something strange the boy doesn't understand. Is it fair play, a knight's code, a biblical translation of a sadistic gesture? Lash LaRue gives back El Azote's bullwhip (No! Don't! Finish him off!)! Now ensues a nasty close-quarters exchange of blows from both men's whips: he flinches each time his hero flinches in pain at a strike on his body. Coming out of the theater he was already thinking about how he'd explain it to the boys. "You see, Lash wants to whip the living shit out of this pile of shit but he will only win in a fair fight, man to man. He risks nothing: the best man always wins."

"Naw," Cliff broke in. "It's—just—a—fuckin—movie s'all."

Cliff found it especially impressive to hear that Fuzzy, cornered at the zinc bar between two henchmen, answered every question with an insolent "Mmebe." Cliff used the non-response for a school week, until he wore it out and reverted back to grunts and mantide mumbles or just the blank stare. His father had been shot dead by a hunter who mistook him for a deer.

"Hey, 'Tard," he let go of Preacher and targeted the old man who was a boy. The rest of the room kept out of this—their business was waiting to hear what he would say. "Me and the boys is havina all-day ball game, so bring your mitt and we just might let you watch us play, mmebe you can even be ump if you don't hurt yourself too bad." The guys always chose him to play the victim. He was smarter but smaller than them, his leg touched by polio, so he read books and ran slower and tired easily, though no one in those days acknowledged the handicap—to them, he was just not a manly boy. A cut above the Negro kid. It was easy for the cowboys to bind his hands and string him up on the clothesline, cast him as the clod-buster burned out by Joe Dillon Indians, place holder for Lou Groza's game-winning kick as the clock showed no time left in Cleveland, baseball umpire without a mask, All-American dumb fuck. They had to invite the old man who was a boy to tag along to the sandlot after he bought a catcher's mitt, the only one in the neighborhood, a Jim Hegan model from the Sears wish book.

**"The White Scar"**

The scar has a history.

Vermillion in his youth, moon white with age, the scar around his neck marked him in society. He develops a fondness for turtle necks when they came into fashion, neck ties, ascots, winter scarves, dickies, and buttoned top buttons; an aversion to locker rooms, swimming pools, undressing before his lovers with the light on. If not for the scar, he'd wonder if he'd ever even been hanged or if he was remembering something that never happened: nobody ever talked about it. The scar has all but disappeared into the wrinkled foolscap of skin that is his old man's neck in recent years, although he is careful to remember where not to shave.

**"And All He Knew"**

The horror of swallowing his own tongue was all. He was slowly choking to death a hundred steps from his mother's kitchen. She would be baking. If he blacked out, it struck him, he could no longer be able to stand on tiptoes. He would die playing at dying. The guys had been playing cowboys (shirts) and Indians (skins) since morning, not even stopping for lunch, whipping themselves into delirium at the bottom of the schoolless sun. He had consented gamely to being tied to the clothesline. They had ad libbed a mock tribal dance a couple times around the T-post—"HOW-wow-wow-wa. HOW-wa-wah!"—and then they'd abandoned him. It was never clear if they'd gotten scared, suddenly aware he could choke to death, or if they were trying to kill him or go for help. No one ever said, and no one, not even his parents, ever asked. No one. Ever. Surely, they must have been watching, stifling their laughter then horror, behind the wisteria. Surely, they were poised to rush back at the last instant and save him and all share a big laugh afterward. To think otherwise, to posit that the boys had deserted him, would have meant he could never talk to them again, of course. He'd recently read somewhere that you cannot actually swallow your own tongue, but he remembers that's exactly what it felt like. The horror of swallowing his own tongue was all he knew then, and all the old man can account for now, 60 years on. It was Preacher who circled back with a kitchen knife and cut him down.

**"The Red Sneakers"**

Soon the Negro boy was taking notes in the darkened theater in his desire to accurately account for all he saw and heard to impress the others with his weekly story-telling and surely, surely win a place among the tribal order of the street. They agreed he should be some kind of a teacher or, better, a preacher and heal drunks when he grew up. None among them knew the errantry of art critics and cinematographers. He was the only boy in Ash Flat who saw every movie that came to the nearest town. When his father made a habit of driving the boy every Saturday the 12 miles to Akron, the boy's life changed for the good. On his way to the Wingfoots practice, he man would drop off the boy at the movie theater, where the boy would sit transported through two films, a newsreel, a cartoon, and especially the serial. The balcony was not integrated. The father smoked in the car both ways, so the boy always arrived home green with a headache the mother ascribed to the unhealthy effects of staring at a lighted screen in a darkened room.

Preacher was always decked out in the very latest in sneakers. But the time he sported the red ones, the guys called him a sissy nigger to his face. He had to keep on wearing the red high-top Keds all that summer. He tried to look tougher by leaving the laces untied to drag across the playground, but that only made Preacher look lost in his new red shoes. His father claimed the red shoes were "burgundy" and what the athletes were wearing this year. Several times a week that summer, Preacher rode his bicycle in circles outside our house, looking solemnly at the pavement, never knocking on our front door, never invited in.

**"Last of the Keystone Cops"**

For a town boy[1] in those days after the war, one big appeal was that a Lash LaRue western looked a good deal like kids at play. The old man sees the Hollywood child's play that was part of the denial in the recess after the war when "Negro" and "colored" were words used by nice folks. White kids made up the fan base for the LaRue movies, comics, and TV shows. But no child actors appeared—no Dickie Jones shared a scene with LaRue, no Sugar Dawn or Brandon deWilde—in any of LaRue's westerns until his TV series, "Lash of the West," when two

1 A townie was a child who was not bused but walked to school.

different boys make cameos in episodes four and twelve. And J.D. Sloane, LaRue's wife Barbara Fuller's godson, is only one of two boys to make the cover of a Lash LaRue comic book. Might be the infantile old man sidekick affords more versatility in the low-budget B-movie industry: Fuzzy is there, hilariously flappable for the kids in the audience; he is also a crack shot, cool under pressure, in a crisis. Might be old Fuzzy is the deadly Keystone Cop.

## 4. The Virginian

It had already been how many weeks? Kent Johnson is waiting for the old man to e-mail the remaining sections of the manuscript and any last-minute corrections so he can at post the promised "Author's Preface to *The Virginian*" for the many readers of his blog. The process requires the old man to venture downtown to use one of the computers at the public library.

...The heroic cowboy—his iconization in the American imagination above scout, explorer, cavalry officer, fur trapper, homesteader, miner, Native American chief, gunslinger, or any other compelling historical figure from the frontier—is the invention of Wister and two of his close friends, Theodore Roosevelt and artist Frederic Remington. The triumvirate learned well their Herbert Spencer catechism at Ivy League schools before turning to the Far West for the testing ground for eastern ideas. The timing was fortuitous, for Frederick Jackson Turner's Frontier Thesis (1893) was then in the minds of Americans. Turner surmised that it was the frontier experience which shaped our distinctly American character. Teddy Roosevelt's four-volume history *The Winning of the West* (1900) endeavors to rationalize westward expansion as a nation's racial destiny. As late as 1910, Roosevelt was still espousing a Social Darwinist vision of America—re-gifting, as it were, Spencer to England—in his Romanes Lecture.

"Let us hope that our own blood shall continue in the land," Roosevelt admonishes his Oxford auditors, "that our children and our children's children to endless generations shall arise to take our places and play a mighty and dominant part in the world." (Notably, Darwin's long-time friend George John Romanes was a biologist!) And it was Remington who had urged Wister to write "The Evolution of the Cow-Puncher," a widely read essay appearing in *Harper's* magazine (1895), in which Wister boosts the working cowboy as heir to the Anglo-Saxon knight.

"No doubt Sir Launcelot bore himself with a grace and breeding of which our unpolished fellow of the cattle trail has only the latent possibility; but in personal daring and in skill as to the horse, the knight and the cowboy are nothing but the same Saxon of different environments, the nobleman in London and the nobleman in Texas."

Among his bags for his first trip West, from Philadelphia to a dude ranch in Wyoming, Wister packed a copy of the cumbersome score for Wagner's *Die Walküre*. Over the course of eight summers cramped into 1885 and 1893, he communed to Wyoming to be in the company of captains of industry and Wall Street Go-Getters, members of the social arm of the Wyoming Stock Growers Association, the Cheyenne Club. Ten trips West in all, his last completed in 1895, and the mythologizer of the ranch corral could scarcely be said to have left the gated community of his eastern experience. When Remington published his own western novel a few months after *The Virginian* appeared in print, it was in part to rebuke his friend for ending *The Virginian* after his New Adam abandons Eden. Remington had first met Wister at Yellowstone in 1893. If there is no more of the historical West in *The Virginian* than there is to be found in a Karl May novel, then what is "the first real western novel" aiming at?

Wister engineered his western hero to personify, in his swift personal "evolution" from shiftless cowpoke to ranch foreman to eastern entrepreneur, what he held to be the perdurable truths of Herbert Spencer's doctrine "the survival of the fittest." Spurred by Spencer's sociology, American Social Darwinists like Wister strategized a politics of fear a century before Trump or the Tea Party. In Wister's day, Spencer hovered over the land like "a whole climate of opinion," as Auden wrote about Freud. Societies evolve, Spencer preached, like animals and plants do: even so—Wister heard the message blowing in the wind—America will evolve in perpetual progress! For good men *("white men!"* the wind whispered), men like the Virginian, will marry good women *("white women!")* like Molly Wood—and in a few generations evil will be extinct. Keep in mind that Wister was writing for a popular readership with a rapacious appetite for its Dime-Novel paperbacks, with its formulaic promise of "the best man always wins," one invested from childhood in the rags-to-riches Sunday school lessons in Horatio Alger fables. In 1902, the year of *The Virginian*'s publication, Herbert Spencer was nominated for the Nobel Prize—in Literature.

The trouble is that Social Darwinism lives on, undead after two world wars and violent cultural wars at home, when today's Americans can no longer hope that history is progress, intrinsic within our politics. Generation to generation, Social Darwinism's DNA has been perpetuated by rote in pop culture approximations of the Wild West, from Ned Buntline's pulp western paperbacks and Tom Mix to Rogers and Hammerstein's *Oklahoma!* and Copeland's *Rodeo* to John Wayne, Clint Eastwood, TV westerns, and Marlboro Man. Agitprop film-maker Cecil B. DeMille recognized *The Virginian* to be a primary American story and became, in 1914, the first of many directors to film it. (Hollywood westerns were a regular feature at Hitler's evening screenings at Berghof; the twisted dictator reveled in their depictions of white supremacy and manifest destiny.) *Quo vadis*, Owen Wister? In 2016, we witnessed the campaign of a hero with Dime-Novel qualifications who was justifiable by superannuated Spencerian rationality encoded in *The Virginian.* Here was the candidate won single-handedly against seemingly impossible odds. Here was the politician who roared: *"I alone can fix it!"* And the maddened crowd roared back!

# 5. Preacher
# "Ghost Has a Laugh"

The old man lived by himself in retirement.

On a Saturday visit to the library when he emailed the latest late installment, he took a minute to order used DVDs from Amazon of all 20 Lash LaRue westerns, plus the two earlier Eddie Dean vehicles which introduced LaRue to audiences. His purchases arrived in the mail by Wednesday morning, except for *The Dalton's Women*, which had to be bought separately, involving a return trip to the library, and would be delivered Friday. He set aside one hour from each day for 22 consecutive days and viewed the films in the order in which they were released. A few times, he must have dozed off during the film, one time his postman knocked at the door so he had to restart it, from the credits, the following day. This rule resulted in 25 consecutive days of viewing. As luck would have it, as they say, he watched *Mark of the Lash* on his eighty-second birthday, reconfirming his opinion that John Cason made the best evil-doer in the series. The old man always consumed a chilled 8.4-ounce can of Red Bull during the hour, never food or snack food. He was careful to take his pill an hour before viewing. He always tried to concentrate his mind for the 50- to 60-minute film. The old man was pretty sure the reels of *The Dalton's Women* had gotten out of order when the DVD was burned, but he pressed on to *The Thundering Trail*. When he had run through all the films in order, he watched his personal favorite again, once a day for another week. The effect of repeated viewings of *King of the Bullwhip* felt to the old man something like teaching *The Ox-Bow Incident* every fall term for 34 years. He never shared a film, with his adult daughter in Oregon or a surviving friend; he always watched alone, turning from 81 to 82, in his library.

He knew it would be absurd to think he could find his boyhood self in these grainy images. He knew the boy was not the one being filmed. On their own, the old man's eyes struggled to match up the slapdash grey black white patterns into some big picture of why the stories had enthralled the boy, what developing muscles the cowboy hero animated. What part childish dreaming plays in our diurnal world.

The old man lived for himself in retirement.

**"Introducing Miss Jennifer Holt"**

The old man decided he really liked the looks of Jennifer Holt. She made, he believed, the best heroine for Lash. She could be mistaken, in the right light, for a young Myrna Loy. Jennifer Holt's early schooling, believe it or not, was at convents in Belgium. He is always disappointed to see that his personal favorite Jennifer Holt was not in every film. He always looked for her. Jack Holt made only one more movie, in a career (like St. John's) dating from silent films, after his role as the banker Kerrigan in *King of the Bullwhip.* The old man was especially disappointed that Jennifer Holt, Jack Holt's real-life daughter, didn't play Jane Kerrigan in *King of the Bullwhip.* He was delighted to see Noel Neill, best remembered as television's Lois Lane, ace reporter for the *Daily Planet* when "Truth! Justice! And the American way!" didn't sound like MAGA propaganda. She radiated energy in her scenes opposite LaRue in *Son of a Badman*. Her WWII pinup ranked second only to Grable's in popularity among GIs. Bing Crosby discovered her in the restaurant at his Bel Mar racetrack and hired her to sing at its Turf Club. Noel Neill, that is, and not Jennifer Holt.

**"Underground Band"**

One day, a student Professor Roe recognized as a campus poet came forward after the lecture and handed him a cassette tape he had smuggled in beneath his sweatshirt. The student supposed rightly that his professor didn't especially keep up with trending popular music, but Roe's recent comments on Eric Fromme had emboldened him to approach the sociology instructor and, for the first time, see him close up. The last night before the professor was sure to see Rich Blevins in class again, he dutifully played the tape, so he could tell him honestly he had. As it turned out, he played the album straight through four times, wonderfully disturbed by what he heard; the singer sounded like a ghost boy. The old man became forever indebted to Blevins, whose gift of *Nevermind* he treasured for a promise that art is greater than the death of youth.

**"Sound Tracks"**

So what does a Lash LaRue western even sound like? The old man found it difficult to write about the soundtracks. The half-hearted attempts by bargain-priced studio orchestras at something sounding "western" range from generic to corny, the most ambitious confined to the credits playing as people find their seats in the dark. Frequently the scores do not seem to fit what's going on on the screen:  a break-neck escape on horseback is half a tune for the buggy moseying to the picnic; a whacky comedic tune bleeds into portents of danger. The spoken word can be a bit off, as well:  the frames are speeded up to make chase scenes faster and fist fights small whirlwinds, the giddyaps and oomphs sound unnaturally high pitched and funny. In short, this ain't no Dimitri Tiompkin. The old man did his homework. Walter Greene, he discovered, composed the musical score for *King of the Bullwhip*. Greene had previously arranged for Harry James' and Xavier Cugat's big bands. He had been nominated for an Academy Award in 1946 for his score for *Why Girls Leave Home*. In the 60s, Greene scored cartoons for Walter Lantz Studio. The boy was aware of none of this; the old man Googled the biographies at the library after standing in line longer than usual, after all it was a Monday.

# 6. The Virginian

Any day now, the final push to the end of the old man's Preface should be coming in. Kent Johnson isn't so sure the fractals fit together to make a publishable essay in the order the old man sends them in or if that was ever important.

...Eighteen-eighty-two, the year Owen Wister graduated Harvard, was a time in need of a general theory for social change. In that climacteric year, Flagler and Rockefeller surreptitiously organized Standard Oil, and Jesse James murdered by Robert Ford. Herbert Spencer visited America in 1882 at the height of his celebrity, a spectacle overshadowed in some circles only by Oscar Wilde's extended lecture tour. Spencer's *Principles of Psychology* was to be found on William James' Harvard syllabi. Yale's resident Social Darwinist William Graham Sumner became the first professor to teach a sociology course. At Johns Hopkins, Herbert Baxter Adams instructed Frederick Jackson Turner and Woodrow Wilson in Spencerian historiography. But there was an innate destructive element in the innovations. And this is the dark side of Wister's novel and Tweet rants from Donald Trump's phone. Wister was taught to believe that democracy bore within itself the latent seeds of its self-destruction. That, even though conditions seemed propitious for a populist hero to rise from the masses and lead, those masses might just as well destroy the Gilded Age Republic. As one cautionary measure, 1882 also marked the passing of the Chinese Expulsion Act, Congress' first legislation to limit immigration into the country. Social Darwinists of the time feared their America was under the threat of "undesirable immigration" by "racially inferior" groups of Mexicans and southern and eastern Europeans; along with organized labor, government feared the new arrivals would mean citizens out of work. Nationalized aliens might sway the vote in future U.S. elections. In 2016, we had "Build The Wall" and Trump's bungling attempts to keep out Mexicans and Muslims and turn back the clock on racism, but Wister is an equal opportunity racist. *The Virginian* smears a sweeping variety of peoples and creeds, including Mormons, Mexicans, Germans, Chinese, African-Americans, and Native Americans, in the guise of cowboy talk. Wister's American myth ignores the multitude of non-white contributions to the exploration and building of the West. Right next to immigration at the top of the list of perceived threats to a Spencerian democracy, what Wister feared most were organized labor and women's suffrage.

At the same time the President Trump is reaching out to befriend the working class in his America First lip service, his administration is acting to emasculate organized labor and workers' rights. Our autocratic executive makes a grotesquely ironic spokesman for working America. In Chapter XVI of *The Virginian*, hired hands, swayed by the Virginian's theatrical lying, vote with their hearts. The cowboys turn down Trampas, whose pitch was for them to abandon their ranch jobs and follow him to make their fortunes in mining. Trampas' news of the ascendancy of mining over ranching *is historically correct and not the "fake news"* decried by the novelist. History tells us that time was running out for the cattle industry, while the mining boom was the next big thing in the West. The men elect against their own interests to stick with the Virginian and ranching, in this way proving the Virginian's worth as a newly promoted foreman. Wister sets his story precisely at the time of the historical apex of the cattle industry and when workers were organizing. That the scene occurs in a railroad car is significant because railroad workers in the West were among the first to join unions. In the wake of the Rock Springs Massacre (killing Chinese migrant miners in Wyoming), the Wabash Railroad Strike, and the Haymarket Riot, all between 1885 and 1886, Yankee Spencerians like Wister feared the fledgling American labor movement was rapidly evolving into what they called a "mobocracy"; in the novel, the anti-union Wister calls Trampas' invitation to the workers nothing less than a "mutiny." Here the myth-maker novelist is dealing in an "alternative fact." Wister is lobbying history, on behalf of his summer companions in the Wyoming Stock Growers Association, and on the wrong side of the Wyoming range wars. During Wister's time in Wyoming (which included a brief stint as acting manager of a ranch), big ranchers were waging a largely legal war against small-time land owners, branding them "rustlers" and land-grabbers. Johnson County juries failed time and again to prosecute independent ranchers who rounded up strays on what they considered to be their own property. Wister has the Virginian hang his best friend Steve for a "rustler," as further evidence of the hero's supposedly Mueller-like virtue. Spun out like another of Trump's 250-digit conspiracy fantasies, Wister's vindication of the WSGA is a rewriting of legal history—his narrative conveniently blurs the definition of "rustler," in the way he earlier redefined "mutineers." By the novel's final chapter, we learn that the Virginian has made a fortune from his investments—in mining! A contemporary corollary might be candidate Trump's promise to revive American steel-making, forgetting his long history of buying foreign steel to build his hotels...

The old man was not a reader of literature, so he could not take heart in remembering the fact that Joyce organized a chapter of *Ulysses*, the seventh, in fractals. And Emma Lazarus—"By the Waters of Babylon." He did, however, during the writing of the Wister piece, refer to notes he had taken as a young man in a Howard Vincent seminar on Melville.

# 6. Preacher
# "Deception Pass"

I hate the seasons here.

It is always the same season in Lash LaRue movies. The filmed desert is well past blossom. The snow is on vacation from the distant mountains. Each day is long with available light, and dusty. Even the day for nights are temperate. Deserts are known to occupy one fifth of the earth. The sand gets into everything, your boots, your nose, even the food you chew. But my post-polio syndrome would appreciate a move to the desert. The sun shines 160 days a year here; the months build up expectations that next month will be unseasonably fair.

And the seasons here hate me.

**"Daughter of the Bad Guy"**

I was shocked to learn from my parents that our neighbor's wife Erlene Powell was the daughter of Earl Horn, the white supremacist who organized Klan meetings on his farm land in our very own Western Reserve—I could detect nary the whiff of a burned cross on her. I always believed Erlene (although the name means "elfin," I doubt Earl cared) remained innocent also of the effect her clinging sweaters and nude stockings had on a male pre-adolescent virgin. I knew her as a childless woman, a decade younger than her husband, who liked to get right down on the carpet and play with my plastic cowboy-and-Indian figures. Erlene of the tight brunette curls had a tick which the boy imagined was sexy: every so often, especially upon finishing a sentence, she audibly sucked on her teeth and smiled at me. She was always staring right into my face when I looked up from her garter flash. One Christmas, she gave me a Smithsonian book on the Revolutionary War; another time, it was a table book of Remington pictures. At 10, I planned to marry Erlene when I grew up and save her from her husband and father. The inscribed books are still in place on the shelves in the old house.

# 7. The Virginian

**Oriana Fallaci Interview with Secretary of State Henry Kissinger**

*HK: Well, yes, I'll tell you. What do I care? The main point arises from the fact that I've always acted alone. Americans like that immensely. Americans like the cowboy who leads the wagon train by riding ahead alone on his horse, the cowboy who rides all alone into the town, the village, with his horse and nothing else. Maybe even without a pistol, since he doesn't shoot. He acts, that's all, by being in the right place at the right time. In short, a Western.*

*OF: I see. You see yourself as a kind of Henry Fonda….* (*Interview With History*, 1976)

…Wister's foreman hero sways his crew by virtue of his tall-tale speech. This is the Virginian at his Spencerian campaign hustings. The unintended lesson seems to be that no Trampas who is in possession of the facts can beat a Virginian who takes charge of the management of news. Wister espouses a leadership by artful deception. The Virginian, as we have said, claims Trampas is bearing false news and counters it with alternative facts (all impromptu afflatus much like the more coherent moments from off-script Trump), concerning an allegorical frog farm industry. In short, he bluffs as only a mythic hero is allowed. The cowhands are made to cheer his bombast with the call: "Rise up, liars, and salute your king!" Wister concludes the chapter with a reiteration of the Virginian's admiration of Queen Elizabeth for her ability to bluff, as in a game of poker. "Don't you think you could have played poker with Queen Elizabeth?" an admirer observes. On the other hand, Wister does not confuse lying for legend-making. Wister is fond of gently comparing the Virginian to George Washington; when the cowboy suitor writes a letter home to Molly's family, his handwriting even resembles the Virginian aristocrat's. But there can be no Parson Weems fable of cherry-tree chopping for Wister's western. When Wister writes his biography *The Seven Ages of George Washington* (1907), he repudiates the Mason Locke Weems' fable, and its perpetuation in McGuffey Readers: "It is a misfortune for all American boys in all our schools to-day, that they should be told the untrue and foolish story of the hatchet and cherry tree." At least as far back in literary history as Homer, the hero is the only one in society who is allowed to lie, and he lies well, as he does all things well, in the memorable form of tall tales. Why, Odysseus' journey may be entirely the machinations of a king's ego. The Virginian is further privileged by the well-tested Dime-Novel formula of tongue-as-weapon: "Frawgs are dead, Trampas, and so are you," he taunts after the frog farm tale.

A president's lies have become a regular feature of the news cycle. *The New York Times* prints updates of its chronology of Trump lies. This torrential fibbing is not the usual political prevarication, misspeak, bull shit, self-contradiction, myth-making, and campaign promises forgot to the expediencies of governing; the issue of this president's lying goes deep into the psychic needs of the compulsive liar to invent reality and always get his way. Wister's cowboy is taciturn, when he is not telling tall tales, the original to Gary Cooper's portrayal of Will Kane. The Virginian always has his way, vanquishing enemies rhetorically: Trampas (with a famous bluff, "When you call me that, *smile*!") and the itinerant drummer early on, then the Rev. Dr. MacBride late in the novel. These foes are guilty of spoiling the silence of the West by their infernal rackets of talk. To us, the villains seem like past masters of a Trumpian periphrasis. The MacBride chapters present a showdown for the Virginian almost as crucial as the duel in the street that will at length revenge Trampas. If MacBride is right in his Father Mapple-like sermon damning all cowboys to Hell, then Social Darwinism in the novel is wrong; a good man could never rise above the rabble.[2] No, the Virginian was meant to provide an aspirational model; whereas, Donald Trump, more MacBride than Virginian, is an anomaly.

---

2 Wister nicknames MacBride "Jumbo," probably not for Mapple in *Moby-Dick*, a neglected book in those days, but more likely after the elephant P.T. Barnum purchased from a London zoo *in 1882*. Note: This is the first of several items the author cannot know, intrusions in the novel you need to know, delivered in the forms of voice overs, editorial footnotes, and marginalia in the library copy.

Donald Trump's conviction is a matter of public record: women in America, at best second-class citizens like Molly Wood, have their proper place. See: "Lock Her Up!", Stormy Daniels, "Hiawatha," and the "Access Hollywood" tape. Wister chooses Wyoming for his novel's mise-en-scène knowing its nickname "The Equality State" commemorates Wyoming's advance in granting women's suffrage. However, we also know that Wister, an apologist for Social Darwinism, feared what change the enfranchised female might visit upon democracy. In Chapters V and VI, Wister has irrevocably linked the pixilated Em'ly ("She is just one of them parables," is the Virginian's non-explanation) and Molly Wood! One might expect only a morbidly sexist man or a Social Darwinist sexist would equate his heroine, a virgin schoolmarm who cared for others' children, with Em'ly, the ranch's spinster hen who committed acts of immaculate brooding—and separately publish the slander for a gentleman's "humorous" short story condemning a woman's right to vote. It is in this same Chapter XII when we witness Molly Stark Wood's de-evolution from primary character into designated mate for the story's natural aristocrat-in-the-making. Wister created Molly Stark Wood of Bennington, Vermont for his novel's leading lady, the "sincere spinster" who could if pressed claim the pedigree of a Revolutionary War family, the kind of "good blood" that would turn on a Social Darwinist. The historical "Molly" Stark, wife of General John S. Stark, has a state park named after her for the active part she played in the Battle of Bennington, on August 1777. An elitist Owen Wister denigrates Bennington to a backwater burg, in denial of the fact that he could trace his own family ancestry back to the Bennington of William Ellery Channing, the Unitarian and Transcendentalist thinker. In fact, Wister's Harvard had been redesigned by university president Charles W. Eliot in part after ideas championed by Channing. And Wister's wife and second cousin, Marry Channing Wister, was an outspoken civic leader in Philadelphia. Her nickname was "Molly."

Molly Wood, functioning as Em'ly's avatar, can only achieve fulfillment in the role of a Social Darwinist breeder, playing the Eve to The Virginian's Adam in the New Eden of the American West as envisioned in the novel's final chapter.[3] As a test before betrothal, however, the Virginian challenges Molly to a verbal showdown by initiating an exchange on the nature of equality in Chapter XII, "Quality and Equality." Molly thinks they are talking at cross-purposes but

3 The publisher's apologies go out to the scholars of the new Darwinian literary studies, who will have to found their theses in the Virginian's acts of choosing his mate, and in the Freudian symbolism of the couple's honeymoon island in the wilderness, like finding a 50-dollar bill inside a book. If the reader discovers the 50-dollar bill later in this book then it is a condition of textual coherence, and might launch new multi-disciplinary studies in U.S. Grant and the printing of so-called green backs in 1934.—KJ.

her suitor maneuvers her into a corner. Gaining a foothold with his seemingly innocuous statement that "All men are born equal," he launches into a concise demonstration that proves the students in her own classroom do not show equal abilities. Molly is trapped and never recovers in the novel. "[E]quality is a great big bluff. It's easy called." The Virginian called that bluff earlier, in Chapter X, in a funny scene. The cowboy and Lin McLean conspire to prank parents back stage at a barbeque by switching around their babies. In the comedic aftermath, the babies' identities have been easily mistaken. Wister's dead-serious message: if we are not born equals, we evolve identities.

Wister's natural aristocrat-to-be is not an equal among citizens. The Virginian, he stipulates, needs to be the more-than-equal: he embodies quality. Wister, having taught the teacher the truth of Social Darwinism and the folly of republican democracy, opens Chapter XIII with an un-novel-like disquisition in the full-voiced language of the member of the Pennsylvania bar that he was in real life. It is as if Social Darwinism were on trial:

"There can be no doubt of this: All America is divided into two classes,—the quality and the equality. The latter will always recognize the former when mistaken for it. Both will be with us until our women bear nothing but kings. That is, on that judgment day when only the fittest Americans are survivors, the verifiably good women will present their good men with a generation of natural aristocrats!"

Wister claims the Declaration of Independence, while never mentioning the Constitution, "acknowledged and gave freedom to true aristocracy, saying, 'Let the best man win, whoever he is.' Let the best man win! That is America's word. That is true democracy. And true democracy and true aristocracy are one and the same thing." Democracy in *The Virginian* is theoretically founded on principles in the Declaration of Independence—without consideration of the Constitution and the Bill of Rights. One cannot help but bring to mind the Trump Administration's repeated assaults on the Constitution and its impatience with the Bill of Rights.

Elwin Charles Roe
Emeritus Associate Professor of Education
Mt. Union College, Alliance, Ohio

The old man sat at the typewriter in the bunker for a long while before he determined to sign his full name to the essay—at length rejecting Charles Roe, the name on his bank checks, and E. Charles Roe, his name in the college directories, the cryptic E.C. Roe and the improbable Elwin C. Roe—and even then there were deliberations concerning the printing of his title—he stuck with Emeritus professor through several name drafts, since it is usual for an emeritus faculty member to retire as a full professor, but that was dishonest and vain and stuck out for posterity like an elaborate headstone for a poor family. These end-game deliberations left him zero time to work on "Preacher" that morning.

"Trump's rhetoric has resurrected the Social Darwinist state of America," the old man wrote in a note to himself. "The president's language has directly inspired a wave of domestic terrorism within the culture of Wisteria." In the same session, he took the following notes from Christiana Silva's "Trump's Full List of 'Racist' Comments About Immigrants, Muslims and Others," but for reasons of his own never incorporated the *Newsweek* article into his Author's Preface:

—On Mexicans: "They are not our friend, believe me. They're bringing drugs. They're bringing crime. They're rapists." Immigrants from Haiti and Africa come from "shithole countries." "Haitians all have AIDS." Nigerian immigrants will never "go back to their huts" once they come to America. 4F-in-Chief Trump calls out a Gold Star Muslim family, Ghazala Khan and wife. Claims Judge Gonzalo Curiel cannot fairly hear the Trump University case because he's "Mexican." In 1970, Trump is sued twice by the Justice Department for discrimination, refusal to rent housing to blacks. Retweets anti-Semitic meme from White House.

—Refers to Senator Warren as "Pocahontas" while hosting Navajo Code Talkers veterans at the White House. Trump enters politics as a birther who claims Obama is ineligible to serve as president because he was not born in the US. Calls himself "a negotiator like you folks" in an address before the Republican Jewish Coalition. Refuses to condemn the neo-Nazi violence in Charlottesville, Virginia: "very fine people on both sides."

—Patrick Crusius, the El Paso Walmart shooter, used Trump's terminology in declaring "this attack is a response to the Hispanic invasion of Texas." Trump continues to refer to an imaginary border invasion two dozen times this year, seven times in under a minute in a fall 2019 campaign rally in Florida.

—Retweets anti-Muslim propaganda videos from hate group Britain First purporting to show a Muslim destroying a statue of the Virgin Mary, a Muslim migrant beating a Dutch boy on crutches, and Muslim men pushing a boy off a building. Retweets false statistics about white homicide victims after a black activist was attacked at a MAGA rally in Atlanta. Claims blacks are "living in hell" in inner cities, repeatedly pointing to Baltimore. Describes Baltimore as "a disgusting rat and rodent-infested mess."

—"You could see there was blood coming…out of her whatever" (describing Fox News host Megyn Kelly). "She was bleeding badly from a face-lift" (describing MSNBC host Mika Brzezinski). "Her mind is shot.—resign!" (tweet about Justice Ruth Bader Ginsburg). "When you're a star, they let you do anything. Grab them by the pussy." (*Access Hollywood* videotape). Believes women seeking abortions should receive "some form of punishment." "'Give me your tired and your poor' who can stand on their own two feet and will not become a public charge," Ken Cuccinelli, Trump's immigration czar, acting director of the US Citizenship and Immigration Service. Dayton, Ohio shooter Connor Betts showed his girlfriend a video of the Tree of Life shootings on their first date.

—The Very Stable Genius tweets about the impeachment probe: "All Republicans must remember what they are witnessing here—a lynching."

—Owen Wister ignores the implications of the July 20, 1889 lynching of James Averell and Kate Watson, on charges of "rustling" by vigilante Albert J. Bothwell. In *The Virginian*, Wister revises the history of the Range War, including the legal definition of rustling, from the point of view of the big ranch owners.

—The worst year for lynchings in America was 1892, when 161 blacks and 69 whites died at the end of a rope.

—In one scene in D.W. Griffith's vitriolic epic *The Birth of a Nation,* Klansmen burn crosses before lynching a black man. In homage, the second coming of the KKK reenact the ritual "lighting the cross" to this day, sometimes by burning a cross-shaped warning into someone else's suburban lawn when the house sleeps.

—In the National Memorial for Peace and Justice, in downtown Montgomery, hang 805 steel plates the size and shape of coffins, one for each county where a documented lynching took place, and inscribed upon the plates are the names of the almost 4,400 African-Americans lynched in the South between 1877 and 1950.

—A noose around his neck from his own harpoon ties Ahab to the whale.

One day the old man tired of seeing the crooked clothesline post on his route to and from the fallout shelter. When he tried to set it straight, putting his weight into it, the T broke off, rusted through just below the ground.

# 8. Preacher "Wingfoots"

I can no longer put off writing "Preacher." I have come to think of it as really a memoir disguised as a novella, so the writing doesn't require a real novelist's understanding of how a novel works. Or how real people work. I simply allowed myself to recall for an hour the childhood stories and soon I fell into the habit of writing them down every morning after I became exhausted from typing my *Virginian.*

They were the only Negro family in town. Their house was a half address, 62 ½ Liberty Street, a prim ranch set behind an old farm house on our street. My parents said Mr. Swyers was employed as a rubber sneakers sales representative but that he never worked a shift in the factory since he played basketball for the Goodyear Wingfoots. Leroy Swyers was a kind of underground celebrity, a local athlete, but nothing like a player for the Celtics or Pistons. I was strictly afraid of him. His chiseled face of bituminous black didn't smile for the camera like Larry Doby's or Luke Easter's: his eyes seemed to smolder with ire. His hands and feet were the biggest I had ever seen. I never saw him wear anything but a bleached white tee shirt, blue jeans, and penny loafers without socks, until the day of the funeral.

TRAINING PAYS DIVIDENDS AT GOODYEAR

*Akron, Ohio – The Goodyear Tire & Rubber Company, sponsor of the Goodyear Wingfoots in the National Industrial Basketball League, has had in effect since 1913 one of the best known and much discussed training program in the nation. Most promising young men who enter the company are placed under the auspices of this program as a member of one of the Goodyear Squadrons – production, office or engineering.*

*Through the Squadrons, Goodyear offers unusual training opportunities to the capable young men who are seeking advancement in industry. Both shop and staff working assignments are accomplished by actual performance of the operations and not by mere observation. This provides the trainee with a natural appreciation of the problems of the individual he is being trained to lead later.*

*Goodyear Wingfoot basketball players fit into this training program. Most of them are or have been Squadron men. As such, their training is a full-time occupation. They receive no added compensation for their work on the basketball court, but they are provided a splendid opportunity to make themselves better known within the organization.*

*The end result is nice to contemplate. In the office of the president sits Edwin J. Thomas, a member of three Goodyear basketball teams in the early Twenties. He often chats with another early Wing star, Factory Superintendent Leroy Tompkinson, and with Vice President Victor J. Holt, 1929 Helms Foundation All-American at the University of Oklahoma.*

*To consider the success and value of the Goodyear basketball program, one need only talk with the many former court stars who today hold responsible positions with the company.*

("Training Program," Release #12, 1954)

**"The Underground Ballcourt"**

Of course, when the Hero Twins, Hunahpu and Xbalanque, played a ball game of Mayan Good versus Evil against the Lords of Xibalba, the demons tricked them, putting in play the nine-pound rubber ball laced with razors. According to Dennis Tedlock, "*jom*, once the Quiché term for a ball court, had become a term for 'cemetery' by the early eighteenth century and remains so today." (*Popol Vuh*, 1985) Sociologists claim the Mayans invented the boxscore and an accurate calendar for tracking human sacrifices.

**"The Story of the Swyers"**

Preacher looked like an even smaller version of his petite mother: his eyes were plagiarized from hers. Dee was a light-complexioned woman, younger than the father. She obviously preferred reading books over house work. That alone was enough to set her apart in our community. Because of her, the family lived among avenues and alleyways of magazines and used books, as if all the reading matter in the town came here to live out the end of their shelf lives. I believe her hands were beautiful, the way they could be chocolate or coffee with cream when she gestured. She caught me looking at them and gave me a look, crossing her eyes and sticking out her tongue for a second. That night, alone in bed with those fingers: white wax melting down black candle. I tried looking up Money in the encyclopedia after hearing her lips pronounce the name of her favorite painter. Preacher's parents had met at some college in Virginia, where he lived on a basketball scholarship and she studied art. She dropped out when Preacher came along, and he quit after his junior year when Goodyear called. At Preacher's invite, I attended Sunday services at his church a couple of times, mostly so I could study Dee in a dress. Salvation Baptist Church wasn't much different than my Baptist church—cooked up the same Old Rugged Cross hymns, the same fire-and-brimstone sermons seasoned by spasmodic outbursts of spontaneous testifying, Amen. the collecting the offering of small change and dollar bills in wicker baskets, the four-part piano-driven Blackwood Brothers harmonies you didn't dare dance to followed by the same endless invitation for wayward souls to come forward and be saved in the blood of the lamb-—but beyond these quiddities, there existed a whole parallel world of difference, the black and white. I didn't make this a practice, and I couldn't reciprocate by inviting Preacher to the strictly segregated Akron Baptist Temple: we would never make it past the armed angels with southern accents who zealously guard the gate as in Salt Lake. Knowing Preacher made me question for the first time the wisdom of the church fathers. I never breathed a word about it to the guys, or the story of the Swyers. I have always been a coward.

Growing up, it's clear to me now, I was something like Preacher Swyers. One of my Sunday school teachers, a Mr. Butterball, favored me for my precocious readings of bible stories. He must have been approaching 60 then, a used-up factory worker with rotten lower teeth and black hair on his knuckles, who wore the same brown double-breasted suit every time I saw him. And so it came to pass, the weekend teacher chose me to deliver a prayer of my own invention at the start of services on a given Sunday morning in the near future. The date loomed from the calendar. It would be my virgin stab at public speaking. I remember nothing of whatever platitudes I must have delivered, no doubt in imitation of Pastor Billington but leaving out the hell fire parts. I remember standing there in front of "the world's largest Sunday school," upwards of 5,000 young souls assembled in what was the original Manchester Road building the Baptist Temple had grown out of; I remember Mr. Butterball crying afterward. This would be about 1947, or the year Lash LaRue hit the movie screens. The year Preacher started giving his recreations of the LaRue stories. Within another two years, I would be driven by the hypocrisy of ascesis and bigotry of the church to declare myself an atheist. I had grown mortally embarrassed to be for a minute longer associated with the old-time hillbilly religion of my family. I was ashamed of my father and mother, although I didn't know it until I was 30.

**"Blood Brothers Forever"**

It was the cutting part and not the blood that put him off.

During their lengthy talks about becoming true blood brothers and the ritual of exchanging blood, the boy mentally set aside the knife to circle endlessly around alternative methods including symbolic red pen tattoos, picking scabs, solemn sips of tomato juice from a shared cup, squeezing hang nails, coincidental bloody noses, mumbly peg, maybe pin pricks. The boy routinely fainted bombs away after penicillin shots. All talk became prelude when the boy was flipping out about a fresh paper cut. Preacher, immediately full of purpose, produced from his desk a miniature baby tooth, crusted black inside and capped by a silver filling. He rubbed its rough end along the boy's cut, popped the thing into his mouth—and swallowed Just like that, the two boys were blood brothers forever, like Jeff Chandler and James Stewart! The shaman "released his grip on the wrists and took the heated blade from the fire. He waved it to the directions and then he plunged it into the earth. 'The blood is the man,' he repeated, 'and the earth is his mother.' He took the still-hot knife from the earth and he cut open the flesh in Cochise's right arm eight inches above his wrist and he held the arm over the silver goblet and let blood flow into it. He took Jeffers' right arm and cut open his flesh eight inches above his wrist and he held the arm over the other goblet and let blood flow into it. Then Nochalo placed their right arms together so that the incisions covered each other and the flowing blood comingled. He held the arms together for several minutes and then he released them and said, 'Drink.' They each picked up the cup which had the blood of the other and drank." Jeffords remembered Cochise as "a man who scorned a liar, was always truthful in all things, his religion was truth and loyalty." (Arnold)

Decades later, the old man read that the mystical Apache ceremony depicted in *Broken Arrow* was bad history, contrived by Elliott Arnold for his novel *Blood Brother.* Literary blood brothers originate in the German westerns of Karl May, one of history's most accomplished pseudomenos and con men, who promoted the autobiographical reading of his fantasy books. Real history, punishment for adultery meant cutting off the accused squaw's nose for example, does not intrude here.

**"Happy Am I"**

When he got up to speed and into his speaking rhythm and voice, when the Holy Ghost was surely in him and speaking through him, when the cloture of his skin was being lost downstream by the river of language, it was then Preacher Swyers became our version of Elder Lightfoot Solomon Michaux, the "Happy Am I" force of nature on the airwaves Saturday nights.

**"Dr. Billington"**

The preacher man first and foremost in my boyhood, and the measuring rod for all the preachers who would follow, was Dallas Billington. (For he who controls the water rights, and the trail through the pass in the rocks to the water, rules this town and everybody in it.)

I loved feeling present and accounted for in the packed auditorium when the preacher would get so caught up in the spirit he'd do his best Billy Sunday—whipping out his big white handkerchief to wipe his brow again, now strutting across the stage with the handkerchief tied at his bulging neck—listening to Billington and staring with unfocusedwideeyes at the River Jordan not rolling from up there but meandering down its ancient way among rocks in the baptistery mural seeping through a holy wasteland, a landscape seemingly devoid of man, until the flow emptied itself into the elevated tub at the back of the open-mouthed choir; mesmerizing myself by staring into the by now dazzling oil stream of the beginnings of a phosphine migraine and listening, as if for the sound of water underground, attempting to experience levitation at the moment eyes lost focus, oblivious to the two camera men filming the hour live from the lip of the balcony over the vast U of the packed auditorium,[4] the saccharine decay of flowers from recent funerals and weddings disagreeing with sweat and starched shirts forming a low cloud from mouthwash and mints exhaled by hymn singers in need of a smoke making my head ache with religion.

**Robert Smithson, "A Cinematic Atopia"**

"Going to the cinema results in an immobilization of the body. Not much gets in the way of one's perception. All one can do is look and listen. One forgets where one is sitting. The luminous screen spreads a murky light throughout the darkness...Impassive, mute, still the viewer sits. The outside world fades as the eyes probe the screen." (1971)

**"Preacher Turns Detective"**

At some point in every service, one old gentleman who had been present no doubt since the church opened would become moved by the holy spirit, shout out "Praise God!" then lapse back into his harmless coma. The Akron Baptist Temple rigorously denounced faith healing, snake handling, speaking in tongues, childhood baptism, baptism by sprinkling, sex before marriage, female clergy, communists, Wilkie Republicans, the Catholic Church, idolatry, abortion, drink, dance, or the mingling of the races.

Dr. Billington was the fount of an endless stream of stories, testimonial anecdotes which peppered his ser-

4 "[T]he new auditorium was covered in the *Encyclopedia Britannica* yearbook of 1950," Billington, *God Is Real*, 1962.

mons. Some of his favorites got into his book *God Is Real.*

"Dead on Arrival" begins: "One fall night, about 2:15, my telephone rang, and a man's voice at the other end said, 'This is Sergeant ______ of the State Police of Medina, Ohio. We have a family here. An ambulance has just brought in a boy who has died in a hanging. The family has told us that they know you. Could you come to the hospital right away?'...The state policeman met me and said, 'In this room is a D.O.A.' The family of the dead boy were down the hall in the waiting room...

"It was the preacher's lot to tell his family that their son was dead. I told them that I had some bad news for them, whereupon the mother asked if her son's condition was serious. Then, like Jesus, who had to say, 'Lazarus is dead,' I had to tell this family the truth...I took from my coat pocket the only comfort at a time like this and read, 'Let not your heart be troubled: ye believe in God, believe also in me.' No poems, songs, or writing which I have ever read have the comfort that the Word of God has in a time of trouble."

"Preacher Turns Detective" (the chapter title is also a caption under the *Akron Beacon Journal* photograph): "The police left me and the attorney alone with the prisoner. We bowed our heads and had prayer. Then I told him the police were not his enemies and would treat him fairly, but that he must cooperate with them. They were just trying to find the murder weapon. They had not told him that the man whom he had shot had died, and when I told him this, the tears came to his eyes...He told me exactly where to find the gun. I went to the place of business where his brother was, and I asked the brother if he knew me.

"I told his brother where the gun could be found, and then I went to the basement. There in the scattered paper and boxes lay the gun. I took a handkerchief from my pocket and dropped it down over the gun. I then wrapped it and put it in my pocket. The detectives had brought me to this place of business, and when they saw me come out of the building, one of them kidded me and said, 'I suppose you are going to tell us you have the gun.'"

**"From the Baptist Hymnal"**

"Onward Christian Soldiers"
Lyrics by Sabine Baring-Gould, 1865, after 2 Timothy 2:3

(1) Onward, Christian soldiers,
marching as to war,
With the cross of Jesus
going on before!
Christ, the royal Master,
leads against the foe;
Forward into battle,
see his banner go!

(Refrain:)
Onward, Christian soldiers,
marching as to war,
With the cross of Jesus
going on before!

(2) At the sign of triumph
Satan's host doth flee;
On, then, Christian soldiers,

on to victory!
Hell's foundations quiver
at the shout of praise;
Brothers, lift your voices,
loud your anthems raise! (Refrain)

(3) Like a mighty army
moves the church of God;
Brothers, we are treading
where the saints have trod;
We are not divided;
all one body we,
One in hope and doctrine,
one in charity. (Refrain)

(4) Onward, then, ye people,
join our happy throng,
Blend with ours your voices
in the triumph song;
Glory, laud, and honor,
unto Christ the King;
This thro' countless ages
men and angels sing. (Refrain to end)

"The Old Rugged Cross"
Lyrics by evangelist George Bennard
(b. Youngstown, Ohio), 1912

(1) On a hill far away, stood an old rugged Cross
The emblem of suff'ring and shame.
And I love that old Cross where the dearest and best
For a world of lost sinners was slain.

(Refrain:)
So I'll cherish the old rugged Cross
Till my trophies at last I lay down.
I will cling to the old rugged Cross
And exchange it some day for a crown.

(2) Oh, that old rugged Cross so despised by the world
Has a wondrous attraction for me
For the dear Lamb of God, left his Glory above
To bear it to dark Calvary. (Refrain)

(3) In the old rugged Cross, stain'd with blood so divine
A wondrous beauty I see
For the dear Lamb of God, left his Glory above
To pardon and sanctify me. (Refrain)

(4) To the old rugged Cross, I will ever be true
Its shame and reproach gladly bear
Then He'll call me some day to my home far away
Where his glory forever I'll share. (Refrain to end)

**"The Burning Lake of Fire"**

"How would you like to go to a place on earth in some isolated city and you're an alcoholic and you just can't quit, or you're a dope addict and you just can't quit, or a woman chaser or a man chaser, and you just can't quit? Your sin is so big they gonna put you in a city with a wire fence around it. They gonna hem you in. They's no dope there; no whiskey; no women. They's no earthly pleasure there…They got a place down yonder. You gonna die. Get your house in order!" (Dr. Dallas F. Billington, live sermon televised from The Akron Baptist Temple, c. 1962)

**"The Functional Shower"**

The old man's father had been told that the steel shelter is lowered into a hermetic vault of concrete much like a casket into its liner for the eternal protection of loved ones. Rest assured, the contractor had told him. The father's goal was to have constructed a box of walls to keep out the dreadful things, but of course the end result was inevitable, only delayed by the walls: mindlessly, patiently, inexorably decay *works from within*, until the body of the loved one is rendered to filthy featureless mire. The son would have been made to shower immediately upon returning from the world and reentering the shelter. The trickle of sacred water dripped on his head is too parsimonious to be called a shower by a Baptist, in the name of The Father The Son and the Wild Goose.

**"Freak Out Shelters"**

My father was freaked out by "Twilight Zone." In episode 68, aired by CBS on September 29, 1961, hysterical neighbors ram in the door to the family's fallout shelter built for four survivors. The periods of intense fist and feet pounding on the hatch have subsided. Silent as the tomb. Now the feeling of being buried alive is overwhelming. We know what's coming, know better than to relent and let them in, once the door is opened for one it would spell the end for all of us. Opened, for which one?

I got freaked out by Floyd Delrose's recent *The Bomb Shelter Builder's Book*. The sub-standard English only made the book seem more credible as I read, as if it was being spoken not written by a neighbor in my hometown. "Of course, any neighbors who watched your shelter be built will be aware of it's existence. This presents an entire laundry list of problems unto itself...as you might imagine. Relationships with neighbors usually fall into one of three categories:  good, neutral, or bad. Even a friendly neighbor can turn on you in a state of panic during an emergency situation. So, unless a neighbor is sharing the financing, planning, and ultimate use of the shelter with you, I would consider all neighbors with any knowledge of your structure into a category of potential threat."

**Paul K. Saint-Amour, *Tense Future***

"Provisioning, burial, outlasting catastrophe inside a hardened bunker:  Time Capsule II expanded the logic of the backyard fallout shelter to the scale of a civilization's informational legacy...[Westinghouse Electric's] Burnham pressed a button to commit it to the earth. Gleaming and torpedo-shaped, the 465-pound Kromarc stainless steel capsule looked like nothing so much as a nuclear missile being winched into its silo [on the last day of the New York World's Fair, 1965]."  (2015)

**"Good Neighbors"**

That night the old man was visited by a nightmare. The agonizing periods of intense pounding of fists and boots on the hatch have subsided. Silent as the tomb. Now the feeling of being buried alive is all but overwhelming. We knew what was coming, knew better than to let them in, once the door was opened for one it would have been the end for all of us. For which one? He pictured the ones who were gathered above him and clawing at the hatch—the boys who had hanged him for fun among them, with their families—until first their hands bled and then the nails on the fingers of their hands were torn off, and still they clawed for admittance. "Blast doors make the ideal hatch, as they bend with the bomb blast then return to shape." He was glad his particular *bigging* wasn't equipped with a periscope: the pitiful spectacle might well have compelled his father in the name of humanity to open the door. Fling open the door to welcome all the contamination from the dead world.

"...once an underground shelter location is discovered, flushing the inhabitants out by blocking air vents or flooding with water is a relatively simple procedure...It is more difficult, and requires more creativity, to conceal the entry and air vents of a personal underground shelter within the landscape of an urban or suburban area. The best way is to cover the entry and vents with something that will not attract the interest of thief's or officials. Perhaps a pile of wood chips, or some dense shrubbery." (Delrose)

In his work that morning, he remembered the decent neighbors (he typed the word "descent") from his childhood who were known to cut wisteria and bring the flowers into their parlors. He had witnessed the old entanglements flower madly then dry up for a long season, seem dead in the land like bigotry and racism, when they were really only dormant and awaiting their time. Cover fire. Writing *The Virginian* taught me, an old man, that nothing is ever really anachronistic in America.

**Brown Notebook Entries on Executions by Hanging**

I am a born insomniac like the mother. I loved to eavesdrop on the parents' pillow talk once they assumed I was safely asleep in the next room. One Sunday night, I lie awake, overstimulated, listening to the father explaining, in that bass cigarette voice, the importance of the hangings at Nuremberg.

Lash LaRue, as Stormy Day, appears in *Wild West*, his second Eddie Dean vehicle, in 1946, the year of the Nuremberg executions.

Executions by short drop method resulted in agonizing strangulations of the condemned Nazis instead of humane broken necks. After 28 minutes, the hangman put a stop to Field Marshall Keitel's groans, probably by pulling down on the swinging body, one eye-witness journalist surmised, or perhaps by wrapping himself around the body and letting his added weight do the job. Hangman Master Sergeant John C. Woods had been court martialed 16 years previously, diagnosed with "constitutional psychopathic inferiority." Woods was accidentally electrocuted to death, 14 years later, while serving with Engineers in the Marshall Islands.

Immediately, the hanged man feels a tremendous pressure on the neck, then intense panic. He is perhaps unable to suffer from the rope cutting into the skin of his exposed neck. Restricted blood flow to his eyes, if they are open, causes tunnel vision. Capillaries in the face and eyes burst. If the neck is not broken by the drop, a slow and painful death by suffocation results, involving the swelling of the brain, which triggers the Vagus nerve at the base of the cranium, reduces the heart rate and blood pressure, and at last stops the heart. Perhaps he does not suffer but exists in a dreamlike state because the brain has released endorphin LSD.

On September 30, 1630 in Plymouth, Mass., John Billington became the first criminal in America hanged for murder. He was found guilty for the blunderbuss shooting another colonist.

President Grover Cleveland served as a hangman when he was Sheriff of Erie in 1872.

The Molly Maguires, militant miners active in the Wyoming anthracite region of northeastern Pennsylvania, which includes Centralia, claimed responsibility for the 1868 murder of the town's founder, Alexander W. Rea, a mine engineer. Four Irish-American were hanged for the crime 10 years later. A year earlier, in 1877, six men convicted of being Molly Maguire members were hanged two at a time on the "Day of the Rope," inside the walls of the Schuylkill County jail. Each condemned man was given a red or white rose to fix in his coat lapel or carry in his hand to the scaffold. The event was heavily attended and widely reported. The historical marker at Old Jail Museum, Jim Thorpe, Pennsylvania, reads:

MOLLY MAGUIRE EXECUTIONS

"On June 21, 1977, four 'Molly Maguires,' an alleged secret society of Irish mine-workers, were hanged here. Pinkerton detective James McParlan's testimony led to convictions for violent crimes against the coal industry, yet the facts of the labor, class, and ethnic conflicts, even the existence of the organization, remain contested. Six others were hanged on this day at the county jail Pottsville; ten more were executed in Pa. through 1879." (2006)

Scholars of the period are quick to liken conditions in north-eastern coal mining settlements to the Wild West boom town.

"As the history of executions in northeastern Ohio unfolded, the execution process became a grim ritual: the same gallows and rope traveled throughout the region for use in hanging condemned men. Despite the law against public executions, large crowds were present at several hangings inside the jail; the crowds were admitted by special passes distributed by the sheriff. Larger crowds gathered outside the jail and sometimes did not disperse until allowed to view the body." (*Encyclopedia of Cleveland History*, Case Western Reserve University Press, 1987)

**Green Notebook**

He was disappointed they'd felt no shock—neither his seat nor his date's had been rigged—but they screamed bloody murder anyhow, for the fun of it. First, the film had appeared to break just as the silhouette of the Tingler crossed the projection beam—the screen had gone dark—all lights went off in the theater except for the exits—then disembodied Vincent Price warning: "Ladies and gentlemen, do not panic. But scream, scream, for your lives! The Tingler is loose—IN THIS THEATER!" On that cue, their projectionist activated the buzzers in the wired seats scattered all around them.

William Castle's Percepto gimmick cost him $250,000 beyond production costs for the surplus airplane wing deicing motors so moviegoers would feel a physical shock.

"He said it seemed as though a movie film were running through his head and that suddenly the film would jam and break, and then there would be only a white light." (Michael Reck, *Ezra Pound: A Close-up*, 1968)

Now I have lived long enough to recognize it was the pure beauty of Dee's hands that put the lie to inequality for me. The bandages were off my eyes. The hands of a painter smeared in colors.

Now the girl informs him—she wants to try the fall-out shelter next! Twice we've fucked in the cemetery. He didn't own a car so no backseat. One time we screwed on a railroad track until we felt the vibration of an oncoming train. I fail to see the irony in sex, the boy confessed.

**"Untouchable"**

Writing this, it seems clear to me how Preacher was like the guy in the story whose buddies smuggle him into the drive-in for free only to leave him back there in the trunk for a whole movie.

There were no Negro girls in our school and for Preacher the white girls remained untouchable, like getting to watch a drive-in movie for free from a convenient hill with no sound. But it is clear that he was the untouchable.

Girls tolerated Preacher with the look of a beautiful pet cat missing a child from a previous home.

**EROTIC ASPHYXIATION**

or the practice of restricting oxygen to the brain to the brink of unconsciousness, usually by a noose around the neck, to heighten sexual pleasure. The colloquial term for practitioners of breath play is "gaspers." This behavior is classified as "paraphilia" in the *American Psychiatric Association's Diagnostic and Statistical Manual*. Highly addictive. The fetish may have originated when it was observed that hanged criminals died with erections. Notably, Peter Anthony Motteux, publisher of *The Gentleman's Journal* and author of "A Poem in Praise of Tea," died from erotic asphyxiation in 1718.

**"Script"**

Fuzzy: "Well, mister, throwin' away my ginger beer is right wasteful of my invigoration."

Decker: "And you're wasteful of my conversation. From now on, get to the point!"

**"Ghost Boy Doubles That"**

Most of the first four minutes of *King of the Bullwhip* are eaten up by longshots of riders—stock footage for "The Scourge" El Azote's stagecoach chase and holdup, for the badly outnumbered Lash and Fuzzy evading Benson's gang of desperados (in fact, Rio's second gang) before they make their entrance into Tioga City, a dusty town that seems strangely familiar. Close ups are reserved for El Azote's bullwhip throttling the neck of the stage driver...bank office and saloon office interiors...the liquor decanter a barkeep pours for a barmaid to take around to a table in a dusty bar that seems strangely familiar. Lash and Fuzzy took the precaution of entering the saloon separately. Fuzzy bellies up to the bar which looks strange and familiar, orders a whisky but dumps the shot into a distracted galoot's beer, the comic reaction of the surprised drinker attracting the unwanted attention anyway of bad cases Rio and Thurmond, who are in the employ of Benson the saloon owner: Rio pulls his gun on Fuzzy—Lash whips the gun out of Rio's hand neatly—a strangely familiar barroom brawl ensues. While Lash throws and takes punches, Fuzzy shows his gun and keeps Rio's henchmen out of the fray—close up of Lash throwing a hook at the camera before his signature coup de grace downcut punch from a 90-degree angle. As a result of the victory, Lash and Fuzzy sell Benson on the ruse that they had come across two dead lawmen and buried them along the trail into town. Benson makes his oily villain's apology and our two heroes retire to the stable to see to their horses. Rio shows up at the stable with his men and, bent on revenge, he shoves a noose under Lash's bloodied nose, threatening to hang him for El Azote. Bank-owner Kerrigan (played by Jack Holt) and his cashier (who we cannot suspect is El Azote himself) hear the commotion and rush to break up the hanging party; Benson too arrives and dismisses his men. "No one would have known they were coming if you hadn't printed the story," Lash confronts the city fathers. "That is, not unless one of you is *El Azote*!" Afterward, Benson, having taken note of Lash's bullwhip, offers him a job masquerading as El Azote—so our boys actually join Benson's gang and are for a time in the business of robbing stages of their gold shipments, in competition with El Azote! A studio photograph from *King of the Bullwhip* shows an unmasked LaRue in the costume of El Azote and posing gun-drawn on a rock shelf above a white horse. He played the villain in the movie's action scenes, actually fighting himself with the bullwhip. In *Frontier Phantom*, the final Lash LaRue western, he plays his look-alike renegade brother. To create his double, all Lash has to do is wear white, ride a white horse, show a temper, and smoke tobacco.[5] PRC studio hired

5 The novelist testifies elsewhere the stink of cigarettes drowned in coffee cups and toiled bowls made him swear off smoking lifelong. That ruled out a professorial pipe for his medical marijuana. His abstemious mother never smoked, he remembered, but her clothes and hair smelled like everyone else's in those days. In the movies the novelist loved, Lash was

Snowy Baker to teach LaRue to use the bullwhip for *Song of the Old West*, his first western film. He chose to wear an all-black wardrobe inspired, he later claimed, by George O'Brien's cowboy outfit in countless David Howard films. LaRue affected a coal-black neckerchief and silver accessories.

**"Gun World"**

*King of the Bullwhip* was C. Jack Lewis' second of many screenplay credits, all westerns but the very last of his career, following distinguished action as a U.S. Marine in World War II and prior to his service in Korea. The founder and co-editor of *Gun World* magazine, Lt. Col. Lewis published a dozen books and some 6,000 short stories and articles. He worked on occasion as a movie stuntman.

---

strictly a non-smoker among the smokers. Fuzzy rolled his own or chewed, like my grandpa, who opened the car door and spit for every stop light.

**"Formula"**

Most of the first four minutes of *King of the Bullwhip* are eaten up by longshots of riders—stock footage for "The Scourge" El Azote's stagecoach chase and holdup, for the badly outnumbered Lash and Fuzzy evading Benson's gang of desperados (in reality, Rio's second gang) before they make their entrance into Tioga City, a dusty town that seems strangely familiar. Close ups are reserved for El Azote's bullwhip throttling the neck of the stage driver...bank office and saloon office interiors... the liquor decanter a barkeep pours for a barmaid to take around to a table in a dusty bar that seems strangely familiar. Lash and Fuzzy took the precaution of entering the saloon separately. Fuzzy bellies up to the bar which looks strange and familiar, orders a whisky but dumps the shot into a distracted galoot's beer, the comic reaction of the surprised drinker attracting the unwanted attention anyway of desperados Rio and Thurmond, who are in the employ of Benson the saloon owner: Rio pulls his gun on Fuzzy—Lash whips the gun out of Rio's hand neatly—a strangely familiar barroom brawl ensues. While Lash throws and takes punches, Fuzzy shows his gun and keeps Rio's henchmen out of the fray—close up of Lash throwing a hook at the camera before his signature coup de grace downcut from a 90-degree angle. As a result of the victory, Lash and Fuzzy sell Benson on the ruse that they had come across two dead lawmen and buried them along the trail into town. Benson makes his oily villain's apology and our two heroes retire to the stable to see too their horses. Rio shows up at the stable with his men bent on revenge, he shoves a noose under Lash's bloodied nose, threatening to hang him for El Azote. Bank-owner Kerrigan (played by Jack Holt) and his cashier (who we cannot suspect is El Azote himself) hear the commotion and rush to break up the hanging party; Benson too arrives and dismisses his men. "No one would have known they were coming if you hadn't printed the story," Lash confronts the city fathers. "That is, not unless one of you is *El Azote*!" Afterward, Benson, having taken note of Lash's bullwhip, offers him a job masquerading as El Azote—so our boys actually join Benson's gang and are for a time in the business of robbing stages of their gold shipments, in competition with El Azote! A studio photograph from *King of the Bullwhip* shows an unmasked LaRue in the costume of El Azote and posing gun-drawn on a rock shelf above a white horse. He played the villain in the movie's action scenes, and is actually fighting himself with the bullwhip. In *Frontier Phantom*, the final Lash LaRue western, he plays his look-alike renegade brother. To create his double, all Lash has to do is wear white, ride a white horse, show a temper, and smoke tobacco.

**"Historical Non-formulaic"**

The U.S. Cavalry camel in the desert is a best example of historical non-formulaic.

**Fawcett Movie Comics #8**

The boy's eye returns obsessively to the ad—

**LASH LaRUE**

**WHIPS**

**LLR-W1: 5 ½ foot**
**braided yarn whip in**

black. (Style as shown in photo above.) LLR-W2: De Luxe Leather Whip.

**"President Reagan's Cowboy Boots"**

"Hand-tooled in gold and silver, these black-ostrich-vamp and cowhide cowboy boots are complete with the Seal of the President of the United States stamped on the front (presale estimate: $10,000 to $20,000). Tony Lama Boots and Western actor Rex Allen gifted the boots to Ronald Reagan in September 1981." (christies.com.)

**"Thirty and Nine"**

Plantation owners would authorize overseers to whip and punish slaves with impunity. The slave traders' mart in Richmond featured a whipping post to which a slave in line for punishment was tied and administered 39 lashes in public. "Men were stripped of their shirts...and women had to take off their dresses from the shoulders to the waist." (http://doesouth.unc.edu.)

**"The Sound in the Movie"**

A bullwhip is a pastoral hand tool designed for controlling livestock in open country. The bullwhip was *rarely if ever used to strike cattle*, as this could inflict damage to the animal. Instead, the cattle reacted to avoid the crack of the whip, the small sonic boom.

**"Genius of the Empty Sack"**

For comic relief, sidekick Al "Fuzzy" St. John added slapstick gestures he'd perfected in studios with his uncle Fatty Arbuckle and Buster Keaton. He could get a laugh out of dismounting a horse from behind or rolling a cigarette. To descend a stairs he might inexplicably squat at the top and open his legs akimbo, straddling an invisible burro into a canyon. Fuzzy might trip over an invisible pebble in the street but, in the next scene, knock a man off his horse with a slingshot.

For comic relief, throughout *King of the Bullwhip* Fuzzy introduces himself with a whopper (such as: "I'm a personal friend of Wild Bill, Pony Bill, and Buffalo Bill..." and "Did I ever tell you about the time I hunted with Buffalo Bill?"), and his auditor moves away every time, leaving Fuzzy's tall-tale open-ended. Following the iconic bullwhip duel, when law and order is restored to Tioga City, Fuzzy, having captured if not captivated his audience, is at last given the chance to launch into his story—the "real" Buffalo Bill shows up—and Fuzzy does a prop swoon to the floor! Such is the fate of tall-tale tellers when reality shows up unexpectedly. The comic book version has Fuzzy declare, "If I'm lying, may my beard part in the middle and my hat jiggle on my head!" This results in a double-frame drawing of Fuzzy Q. Jones' split beard.

For comic relief, Fuzzy obsessively scribbles limericks through *The Fighting Vigilantes*; "Like Preacher taking notes in the theater," thinks the old man.

Al St. John's last film was released in 1952. Working in a traveling Wild West show in Georgia, he died of a massive heart attack while waiting to go on, January 21, 1963.

All the way back in *Law of the Lash*, Fuzzy's first pairing with LaRue after playing sidekick to Buster Crabb, St. John seemed fated to fill the empty grocery sack of the western with delightful formulas.

Fuzzy: "Hey, here's an empty sack, and here's a list of what to put in it."

Lash: "Fuzzy, your list is just like a letter: it always starts out the same way."

Fuzzy: "Oh, you mean sort of, 'Dear Sir'?"

Lash: "No—'Six plugs of chewin' tobacco!'"

**"Digression Turns Out To Be the Narrative Structure"**

The old man set aside his consideration of the form the B-western takes when it struck him—the B-western itself is a digression *in his own life.*

His appearances in a series of exposures, each one exposing little more than the reflective surfaces and his native ability to stay on a horse, in spite of his never being accomplished at delivering words written expressly for him he always, from the very start, looked the part, tacitly understanding the code of the West is never to be written down like accountants' books or cattle brands, and the heroic formulas in Homer were designed for generations to remember. So it was that the boys were taught to believe that evil will be contained, justice is only a matter of an hour, that evil is not sheltered within us.

**"An Act of Vandalism"**

There has been a mistake in Preacher's retelling. Two killers are in hot pursuit of Lash and Fuzzy, so—from his horse Lash climbs the overhanging limb of a convenient tree, lets Fuzzy ride on ahead down the trail with Black Diamond in tow, lets the lead rider pass underneath him then uses his whip for a lasso and pulls the second rider to the ground, beats him in a fistfight; meanwhile, Fuzzy climbs a tree too with some difficulty in order to pull the same trick on his rider, neatly lassos him but the bad guy never hesitates just drags the hapless Fuzzy behind him on his buckskin ass across the desert floor! The Negro boy realizes he's been describing scenes from two other movies but the guys seem to be loving it so he continues.

"Yeah? Well, it so fuckin' happens I was at the Norka yesterday. And I didn't see you there. And I sure as hell didn't see the picture you've been tellin' us about. As a matter of fact, there wasn't no Lash fuckin' LaRue picture that whole entire matinee."——-"The lying sissy! String him up!"——-"String him up! String him up!"

Then Cliff turned on me. "I think maybe LaBoy and Fuzzy Q. are queer for each other. Fuzzy Queer cowgirl... Are *you queer too, sissy*?"——"Hey, Nigger-Lover! Who's your boyfriend?" All of them laughed with Cliff.—— "String them up! String them up!" It was fun to chant together.

Somebody wrote "NL" in magic marker in the pocket of my catcher's mitt. I told my father the letters stood for National League. He wanted to believe my explanation and didn't pursue it, even after one of them spray painted "NL + N" in red inside a heart on our sidewalk. He reported an act of vandalism to the town cop.

**"The Cottonwoods"**

DANNY TYLER

Well, I still say what are you going to do with it? Stealing that thing was a mistake, Jar. Nobody here is interested in a stupid rock and, sure as hell, she'll miss it when her dog goes outside to pee on his nice rock and it isn't there. Widow Young will send out somebody to look for it, and they'll find—us!

JIMMY JARMUSCH

Relax a little, can't you?

DANNY TYLER

Who's not relaxed? Got rocks in your head?

JIMMY JARMUSCH

This here is 100 percent western flint, straight from the Black Hills. Maybe I'll just take my time, chip away at it, and turn it into my very own homemade arrowheads....

GIL CARTER

What you going to do with arrowheads? Fields around Mound Hill Cemetery are always coughing up fucking arrowheads. Every cow path grows arrowheads like dandelions after a good rain. Highest point in the graveyard is the Mound Builders' burial site—dig there beside Harriet Wilson and you'll get a shovelful of flints and Indian bones.

ME

Sure. And crazy Paul Abbey up in Home will sell you a cigar box full for nothing.

DANNY TYLER

The only reason arrowheads mean something is they're ancient, see, not plagiarized by some kid in his parents' basement.

ME

Lucky for us you don't want to sculpt a fucking meteorite!

GARY IKLES

I vote we weigh you down with your rock, Jarmusch, and toss you out into the middle of Chippewa Lake.

GIL CARTER

Or Blue Hole…

DON MARTIN

Problem is, if we just leave it sit here by the campsite, my dad will figure what's what, comes time to plow.

GIL CARTER

…I say Jar lugged it out here, like the dumb fuck he is, and he can just carry it right out again in the morning and put it back where it belongs.

GARY IKLES

Why wait till morning?

ME

You're interested, Jar, I could give you for cheap that big hickory stump Mom's always after me to pull out of our yard. Lots of good whittling for you there. A real Rushmore.

JIM JARMUSCH
(Emits a loud burp to everybody's laughter.)

DANNY TYLER
For that matter, what wagon train took Fern Young West? Since she finally retired from Latin teaching, I hear she keeps pretty much to home training her butt-ugly toy bull. Taught him to shit in her commode, if you please, and wipes his ass afterwards.

JIMMY JARMUSCH
(Emits an epic belch to general censure.)

DON MARTIN
Je-sus! Bring it up again and we'll vote on it, you—

JIMMY JARMUSCH
Fuck voting. (Lights a fart.)

GARY IKLES
The chair recognizes Mr. Eisenhower.

DANNY TYLER
Commie pinko bastards.

PREACHER
Stallin'?

ME
My grandpa is the only farmer—

PREACHER
Farmer.

ME
—the only farmer in the county of Medina voted for Stevenson. Twice.

PREACHER
All the way with Adli! We like Ike!

GARY IKLES
Shut up, Preacher. Put the both of them together and there wouldn't be enough hair for one good haircut, Stevenson or Ike.

DANNY TYLER
Fuck fucking politics anyway, we're camping out. Give me another beer.

GIL CARTER
—Or whatever Dollar calls this cow piss he bought with our good money.

PREACHER
Money!

DANNY TYLER
Here goes nothin. Hey, whatever happened to good ole Clifford anyway? Anybody? Where's he tonight?

GARY IKLES

Dollar has a life, Tyler. (Stage whispers:) Shhh! He's on a d-a-t-e. With a girl.

ALL

(Chorus) A G-I-R L !

ME

That's only because Dollar's old enough to be my father and still in eleventh grade asking seventh graders to the drive-in.

GIL CARTER

It's because he's the only one of us who can grow a mustache. Attracts girls. Not so much the hair between his eyebrows.

GARY IKLES

Jealous much? None of you sisters has to shave more than once a week. Only beard you have is on your nut-sacks.

JIMMY JARMUSCH

Aw, Dollar's home jacking off in his mother's bathroom.

ME

Yeah, you know I did notice somebody's swiped my tweezers and magnifying glass....

PREACHER

You mean binoculars.

JIMMY JARMUSCH

Nope, "Schoolboy Rowe" here brought his Army Surplus binoculars all the fuck the way out here to the boonies to watch the stars tonight.

ME

Asshole, binoculars can't magnify stars; not even a telescope can.

GARY IKLES

Thank you, Mister Science, for that clarification. Duly noted, and don't forget to fuck yourself.

For your information, Dollar's seeing the oldest Ripple girl, Penny.

GIL CARTER

Molly.

JIMMY JARMUSCH

Hey, Roe, how's about let's take turns with your binoculars looking in Molly Ripple's bedroom window?

DANNY TYLER

Is that Molly, or is the Goodyear Blimp landing?

PREACHER

Moon rising.

DANNY TYLER

Dollar in his old age surely has developed the taste for little girls with big asses.

PREACHER

Taste!

GARY IKLES

Cliff ain't here, or you wouldn't talk like that. Cliff ain't here, so why go on about him?

(Ikles was doing a pretty fair job of sounding like Cliff. The big difference was, no one was afraid of Gary Ikles.)

JIMMY JARMUSCH

Somebody *please* take this cigarette away from me, stop me before I kill again—

I've already burned a hole in my shirt.

PREACHER

If Cliff were here, he'd say "If you caught on fire I wouldn't piss on you to put it out."

GARY IKLES

Feel free, Jar, go ahead and burn that stinking shirt you wear every day. Get the fire going while you're at it. What Girl Scout laid this fire?

DON MARTIN

Lindsey Luplow has by far the sweetest ass in school.

DANNY TYLER

Luplow's a stuck up bitch too good for a slob who doesn't go out for football. Perfection, I will grant you, from behind but when I look into her face—I see her brother Al!

ME

Precisely. You know, Tyler, you're beginning to look a little like Lindsey Luplow in this light.

Noticed in gym class you're developing man tits too.

GIL CARTER

And you are beginning to sound more than a little like a homo, Homo. Don't put your sleeping bag on Roe's side of the fire, boys.

JIMMY JARMUSCH

Jesus, how many beers *you* have, Carter? Cut 'em off, barkeep. Closing time. Last drink.

PREACHER

A sasparilla, please.

DON MARTIN

All this fine philosophical debate and to think, we're just warming up. Anybody think to look at that moon coming up over the fields? Indescribable. The kind of summer night doesn't seem real come New Years.

ME

Now look who's the philosopher. Martin, the farmer philosopher. Want these binoculars?

We seven talked until the moon went down—of sisters' toilets, cars and road directions, sexy song lyrics, UFOs and alien abductions, notorious crimes and war stories, dirty jokes and silly jokes, dead presidents, bestiality, Dracula v. Frankenstein films, amazing catches of the baseball and dumb luck catches, Stan Musial v. Ted Williams, air disasters, food no one should ever eat, why it is that Nazis had the coolest uniforms, and then I treated them to 20 minutes of *Pym,* which they'd never heard tell of.

(Following a lull in the talk, we flew out from behind the moon:)

PREACHER
Sshh. Hear that? Hush.

DAN TYLER
Yeah, it's your momma calling: Supper's rea-dy, baby!

GARY IKLES
You hear things.

ME
Leave him be. What do you think you heard, Preacher?

PREACHER
Mine subsidence.

(Without his notes to rely on, or when he wasn't in the spirit, Preacher could be pretty much inscrutable. Like an actor between scripts. He kept it short, knowing the guys would out of the dark cut him off with a rude usher's flashlight in the eyes.)

DON MARTIN

Gets so quiet out here you can hear the town go to bed and bats eating bugs like popcorn at the Saturday movies.

GARY IKLES

And scared little boys peeing their Sunday panties.

Let it get good and dark before I told them my campfire story. Tossed brush and sticks onto the fire so it flamed up and obliterated everything including the stars, making it the center of the boys' existence:

You all know my Uncle Mike. The one who came back shell-shocked from heavy action in the war, failed at drinking himself to death, then taught himself to use a draft table and designed big construction shovels for Japanese companies. Well, Mike was staying in a hotel in downtown Cleveland for a couple days so he didn't have to drive back and forth from Seville. For the cost of the gas he'd have put in his car, Mike figured the room was for free. Here, I tossed brush and sticks into the fire. The desk clerk, a boy about college age, hands him the key to Room 123, just fine. On his floor, the second floor, he passes a door with no number on it so, just for the hell of it (and also because he's the engineering type and thinks about things in an orderly fashion), Mike re-counts the numbers on that side of the hall: 111 by the stairwell, 113, 115, 119, 121, then his 123, and so on out of sight around the corner. Mike takes pleasure in talking to people and in the morning he asks the new desk clerk about the numberless room. I tossed part of a limb into the raging fire so they had to scoot back a little or get their eyebrows singed. The cute middle-aged clerk conspires to inform him, in a low sexy voice in his ear after she looks around the lobby to make sure they were alone, no one is ever allowed to go into that room. Neither guests nor hotel staff. Maybe Number 117, let's call it shall we, is for storage; maybe it's filled with step ladders, extra furniture, and floor polishers? No, no one ever goes inside, no one comes out. I tossed the rest of the limb into the conflagration. Telling the story made me feel strangely emboldened, I had after all mesmerized them, every red eye fixed on me, but at the same time unstable, temerarious like the village idiot, I later thought, tossing live bullets into the fire—I knew the details of the story would explode at the end. When Mike returns from a long day of meetings capped by a formal dinner, his curiosity overcomes him. He has been working at the mystery of Room 117 all day in his head. Mike stops in front of the seventeenth door, drops to one knee in the empty hallway, and spies through the keyhole....I tossed in a whole branch, leaves and all. Inside is a room that looks like a carbon copy of his own but with two striking exceptions. The room is entirely white: walls, ceiling, drapes, carpet, bedclothes, everything. And across the white bed a drop-dead gorgeous naked woman, her statuesque body pallid as a pillar of salt, is reclining. Her white arms are extended above her pigmentless head of trailing hair; he guesses by the ecstatic expression on her face she is in the throws of a spontaneous orgasm. Out of shame, and suddenly realizing his place in the public hallway, he manages to tear his eyes away from the keyhole and locks himself into his room for a sleepless night. Here, I excused myself from the circle and came back out of the darkness with big handfuls of combustibles and green weeds. Next morning, Mike makes it safely past herdoor and tries to concentrate on his meeting, but all he "sees" is the naked girl with the most perfect pale skin he has ever seen. That evening, instead of retreating to his room he can no longer resist, drops to his knees and looks into the room through the keyhole. But this time, all he can see is—red. I don't mean goddamned red walls, red ceiling, red drapes, red carpet, red bed. Not red lipstick he wants to kiss gone. Red. Just red. I throw in the last of the crap—and consider for a feverish moment tearing down one of the farmer's fence posts—instead, I clap the dust from my hands. Well, my uncle Mike freaks out, the unflappable combat veteran scrapes his jaw off the floor and runs the flight of stairs down to the lobby, where he demands, in no uncertain terms this time, that a different clerk at the desk, an old man this time, tell him what's going on with the unnumbered room between 115 and 119. The old desk clerk had been with the hotel, starting as a young bell hop, since it opened its doors to business 70 years ago. My congratulations on your long career, but what the fuck is the deal in your 117? Sir, that particular unit has been left unoccupied since 1938, when the unclothed body of a local gangster's girlfriend was found dead on the bed where she was accidentally strangled to death during sex. I took a cigarette and lit it in the raging campfire, although I don't smoke. I made red tracers in the night air. I'm the one found her, not a mark on her body except the fingerprints at her neck. Sad, I can see Edith Lot's wide open eyes as if it happened yesterday instead of long ago. She was the rarest of beauties, I can tell you, an exotic albino African...that face was in all the papers for a week...And THE ALBINO'S EYES WERE RED!

With that, Danny Tyler became so sick we had to drive him away from the campfire and our sleeping bags. He sheepishly returned after quietly emptying himself of the first beer he had ever tried. Tyler was a gamer no doubt. Puking his head off without whining about it raised him a peg in our society, and he was happy to have it over with, like an aquaphobic baptized at long last. We did not miss the opportunity, however, to stick Danny with a nickname, Red. No other casualties to report; although the tobacco vapor and alcohol fumes, the layer of vomit on the wildflowers, gave me a secret headache to nurse while I basked in my newly won eminence as a story-teller to rival Preacher. I pressed my palms into my throbbing temples, in imitation of the posture of a louche clasping his hands behind his big head. I had only to think of my bovine cousin. Of course, no one but me could appreciate what a dead-perfect acting job I'd done.

When all the beer had been pissed away into the night, and every cigarette burned and thrown in the fire, it must have been after 2 in the morning: the troops badly needed to move.

You hear the creek before you see it and then, looking, the river sound diminishes to ambient.

A girl in a cowboy hat speaking beside a fireplace and a painting of a river in a movie. The girl in a cowboy hat speaking beside the fireplace and the painting of the irradiated river in the movie.

The boys took the trail the old man when he was a boy'd blazed on solitary hikes through the three fields to the cliff above the creek. He knew every boulder, sink hole, fence post, pop bottle, birds' nest, like keepsakes among the furniture in his room. The walks were daily except during the weeks of hunting season when a kid without a gun had no business in the fields. One summer, the fresh carcass of a dog was in his path where it had not been the day before, and the boy's lesson in animal anatomy commenced as he returned to encounter the decomposing corpse. The boy couldn't recall encountering a dog on the trail so far from houses; a big dog like this one would be missed in the community; maybe the dog was old and sick and its owner took him for a last walk and put him out of his misery out here away from the family. The ghost boy was always there before him, standing by the corpse. At first, it was still a dog, it even looked alive, its short brown and black fur rippled in the breeze simulating breathing, but for its headless neck. By the weekend, the abdomen inflated to the size of his catcher's mitt. On the seventh day, he hurried to the spot right after school—the stomach had exploded into a pulsing mass of maggots he couldn't stand to look at—he held his breath. For another week, salvage beetles who dismantled and removed from the carcass every last thing of value. Three weeks in—the white spine zipper and a pocket of hair. In the movies, the headless dog would disappear before his eyes in a time-lapse sequence artfully reversing earlier footage of a flower opening to the sun, leaving a certain impression in the viewer's mind.

Strolling boldly down empty Main Street turned out to be an eerie experience, for me that morning felt something like the aftermath of the nuclear attack, or more recently more like walking into a movie of a ghost town. We found nothing there but buildings that had strangely ceased to function, houses that looked in the twinkling of an eye abandoned. We looped back from unknown Maria Stanhope's grassy triangle before we broke into the school building, through the shop window behind the bushes, inched down dark spooky halls suddenly unknown and walked out, past the case of tarnished trophies our grandfathers won, right through the front doors! Nobody touched a thing or, as if in silent agreement, spoke—only Preacher seemed animated, incessantly shining his dad's 5-cell flashlight, never tiring of making sleeping objects jolt briefly to life—that is, until fuck face Jarmusch carried off Fern Young's rock (perhaps creating a parallel universe). The three-mile hike into town and back to camp only tired us out—Jar had carried the illicit rock, which was about the size and heft of a bowling ball, so he was worst off—in the movies this is the time for the walking dead to return to their graves. The boys stayed more apart now, as if the vast starry night had shrunk their campfire.

I walked away from the fire to get a look at the craters of the pimply moon through my binoculars. I watched for as long as it took for one particular crater to be almost imperceptibly turn from a crisp circle to a C to invisible. The change was more dramatic, and easier for me to assimilate, if I looked away for a few minutes, but the changing crater was more a part of my adolescent life as long as I kept staring at it. I learned, years after that night, we had walked the route the search party took. At Medina County Commissioner William Eyles' direction, 400 men struck west from town center, one man stopping every 16 feet until they formed a line extending a mile into the Western Reserve wilderness. As planned, brass horns blasted from the end of the line signaling the advance north in search for Sylvia Beach, 23 years old and deaf since childhood scarlet fever, "lost in the woods," March 1824, "and never found."

Of course, it got even darker, black as a coal mine if you allowed for the occasional airplane's blinking lights. And yet no boy was willing to be the first to surrender to sleep until Preacher, who had become quiet as the grave, slipped out of the circle and crashed on top of two zippered sleeping bags. After a while, I faked a bathroom break and covered him up with one of the bags.

"We'll get the bad guys after breakfast, Fuzz."

Then it was only Jimmy and I left, and we let the fire dwindle to hot coals. I could no longer make out his face. In Haycox's books, violent fist fights were always staged inside rooms with the lamps extinguished. I had punched Jimmy in the face in anger once, then walked all the way across town to apologize. I found I had to adjust to hear someone near me speaking without being able to see their facial expressions, like people talking over the newfangled telephone for the first time in their lives.

Jar fell asleep mid-sentence in the prolonged dawn when the birds stir and it's always the easiest hour for insomniacs to sleep. I kept watch, letting them doze like rustlers.

Unprepared for the campout to be over, I willed the movie for once not to end. I sat horrified at the prospect of the blank white screen, a specter I myself had raised. Unstoppable first rays of the new rising sun bounced crazily off Fern Young's ornamental flint, transformed into a prop left over from the filming of a western, right into my bleary eyes.

**"The Spirit of Akron"**

The hangar Goodyear built off 224 for the blimp was so enormous, they told us, it made its own weather inside.

Summers, at odd times, we could see the Goodyear Blimp. The newspaper called it The Spirit of Akron. From a distance, the ship was the shape and color of a nail's lunula. It just sat there for hours in silence, a small sparsely inhabited planet new to our sky. And when we got used to its being there, whenever we looked up, it had disappeared.

**"Treasure"**

Relenting, mother made out a check for $1.13 to Western Adventure, I mailed it to Box 1805, Charlotte, North Carolina, and I waited three year-long weeks, going to the post office starting a day after mailing my order. I nonchalantly produced an equestrian Lash LaRue pen knife and my pristine copy of Fawcett Movie Comic No. 8, an adaptation of the film *King of the Bullwhip*, and stood back proudly as the guys went berserk over it. Preacher didn't even look at the treasures. I had mortally wounded Preacher, usurped his tentative position with the gang, never realizing until I did it I would feel sorry. I'd seen the look on his face once before, when the biology teacher marked a big fat D on his report card, right in front of the whole class, because Preacher couldn't bring himself to dissect a formaldehyde cat, and he had to walk back to his seat. For some reason, Lash's horse Black Diamond is named Rush in the comics. Fuzzy does not appear in the Lash LaRue comic book series until number 82, and then as a stableman. These discrepancies in the fantasy disappointed me and turned me against the comic books.

"**Draw!**"

As a kid, I dreamed of becoming a professional artist, before I realized I had no special talent. I have recently come across evidence that I executed hundreds of pictures, years of daily pencil drawings in homage to my boyhood hero Lash LaRue. I unearthed them of late among my mother's papers; she seems to have kept everything. Her son could rudely replicate the black hat and gun belt unfailingly, sometimes catching a fair likeness of the Bogart face, always relying on the heavy eyebrows (like two storm clouds clashing) to pull it off. But I could never learn to draw a horse, anatomical or expessive, on the gallop or at rest, much less an equestrian pose. My childish horses are always flat, too tall or too short, for a rider. The LaRue portrait series, as it were, gradually morphed into ink sketches (thanks to my father's fountain pen) of cow towns and studio reconstructions. The static horizon of temporary buildings and false fronts was given a couple inches at the top of my page—but a formicarium world of frontier enterprises was going on at break-neck speed *beneath* the prairie floor in gold miners' tunnels and cavern rooms. For picture frames, I laid in spurs and saddles, tin cups and tin stars, blazing campfires and greasy cards, brands and barbed wire, ox skulls and buffalo horns, bone dice and shot glasses, lassos and nooses, bat-wing doors and tumble weeds, neck kerchiefs and a necklace of glacier-studded peaks, eagle feathers and arrowheads. A coin with a hole shot clean through it and a cactus housing a bird's nest. One elaborate gun belt and holster occupies two corners of a picture.[6]

**"Motion Picture Frame"**

An arrow moving is motionless, is Xeno's argument, because time is composed of nows. The movie strings together static pictures of nows we see as the arrow in flight.

**"The Etymology of 'Cowboy'"**

Strange to say, it wasn't Atomic Age technology put Preacher's brand of tall-tale telling out of business. When Lash LaRue finally made it to TV, one of the boys' families owned a television set. None of us saw "Lash of the West," 15 minutes airing Sunday nights at 6:30 on ABC starting January 4, 1953 and pulled 12 months later. Late in my routine research for "Preacher," I ordered the show which had been lovingly pirated by <uncle_waldo_in_person>, a retired eBayer my age. (Typed on the personalized DVD case: "Lash LaRue played a modern lawman who reminisced about his grandfather. These flashbacks were mostly clips from old Westerns that Lash had starred in during his Hollywood heyday." Inside, a note to the buyer: "As stated in the listing, THIS IS NOT A RETAIL SET

6 The author is innocent of Munch's sperm borders around portraits.

nor a COPY OF A RETAIL SET as no such thing exists. Although not perfect, these are the best quality episodes available in the collector arena....") I slide in the first of his two discs, no expectations. This is just so I could say I'd covered all the ground I could. Marshall (sometimes rancher) LaRue, wearing the costume of jacket and tie, is asked by a kid or an old-timer to explain some small point relating to his grandfather's West (i.e., the etymology of the word "cowboy"); Lash looks into the camera, destroying the fiction of the marshall's office or the ranch office to talk directly to us out there in TV land. Routine research, just before you turn off the lights in the archive and go home. A dozen minutes of mostly violent action from old LaRue films follow, as if he were illustrating his story, everything ending with a cliff-hanger tease for next week's thrilling episode. Inside of the first hour, it hit me—

THIS IS THE WAY I AM TELLING PREACHER'S STORY!

The mini-episodes, indeed the whole TV series, are precisely the way I had fallen into telling Preacher's story. A narrative by default. Discrete odd bits and pieces culled from whole movies and fit rudely into a new story, or a slim excuse for a story, all the little bits spliced together but telling what they could remember. Dug up from the film vault, respooled, and brought into the light.

In this light, "Preacher" seems to me like that prose home movie Zooey talks about in his story.

**Notes on the Close of the Frontier (Orange Notebook)**

Following the success of *King of the Bullwhip*, Ormond "directed" *The Vanishing Outpost* (1951), an assembly mostly consisting of footage from four previous Lash LaRue westerns: *Mark of the Lash* (1948), *Son of Billy the Kid, Outlaw Country*, and *Son of a Bad Man* (both from 1949). The studio's press book for *Vanishing Outpost* furnishes an advance press release—blanks are left for the theater or newspaper to fill in times and locations—headed "Lash LaRue Shoes Own Horses."

The last B-westerns were made in the mid-50s. Producer and star Johnny Carpenter's *I Killed Wild Bill Hickok* may be the last. Carpenter (not to be confused with filmmaker John Carpenter) was a friend of Ed Wood's and played baseball in the Southern League until a broken leg ended his career. His Heaven On Earth ranch, in Glendale, was devoted to handicapped children.

**"Conscienced"**

The old man knows he needs to confess. He is consumed in old age by the necessity to confess his part in the ancient crime. Equally, in his attempt to erase his guilt, he feels it is killing the boy all over again to bring him back into a world that has gone on without him for 60 years. The statute of his limitations as a man. To tell the secret would betray the other boys who are by now dead or in their dotage. At other times, he feels he is making up a character for a novel.

**Walter van Tilburg Clark, *The Ox-Bow Incident***

"You are mixing things," I interrupted. "I never heard you mix things before. And it was not Shorty's mistake."

The Virginian showed momentary interest. "Whose then?"

"The mistake of whoever took a fool into their enterprise."

..."Was it him I was deserting? Was not the deserting done by him the day I spoke my mind about stealing calves? I have kept my ways the same. He is the one that took to new ones. The man I used to travel with is not the man back there. Same name, to be sure. And same body. But different in—-and yet he had the memory! You can't never change your memory!" He gave a sob.

It was the first I had ever heard from him, and before I knew what I was doing I had reined my horse up to his and put my arm around his shoulders. I had no sooner touched him than he was utterly overcome.

"I knew Steve awful well," he said.

Thus we had actually come to change places.

**"Saint Steve"**

The hanging of Steve and the two rustlers, which occurs an hour into the 1946 film, registers the melodramatic climax of *The Virginian* (Joel McCrea is the Virginian; Brian Donlevy is Trampas) based on the 1929 film (Gary Cooper is the Virginian; Walter Houston is Trampas) based on two silent films (the first, in 1914, directed by Cecil B. DeMille) based on the 1904 stage play co-authored by Wister and Kirke La Shelle. The old man treated himself to a DVD of the 1946 version, a film he had seen on the big screen as a kid. Now all the actors appear to him very well scrubbed and newly laundered. Sonny Tuffs' Steve is a sidekick as martyred saint (recreating Richard Arlen's Steve from the 1929 Gary Cooper/Walter Houston *Virginian* except for the doomed Arlen's singing of "Bury Me Not on the Lone Prairie," a tear-jerker along the lines of LaRue's "Bury Me With My Boots On" in *Song of the Old West).*[7] Now the film ends abruptly, it seems to the old man, after Trampas gets his—not so much a showdown in the streets as the result of a preemptive ambush backfired—there is no time for the New Adam and Eve to honeymoon in the New Eden, only for riding off into the sunset. Now the western town is so neatened up that the dust that blows in the street looks out of place: a filmmaker's awkward visual reference to the clean metaphorical "wind" from Trampas' shot that nicks the Virginian's sleeve in the book; an empty Hollywood thing at length, devoid of the original political messaging, now the visual demonstration of what Owen Wister's story was all about, meaning Wister's quest for meaning never did have to be the truth.

**"Within the Belly of the Beast"**

Every day, the old man enters the fallout shelter and works on the two manuscripts. He retypes the story of the cowboy hero beside the story of how the Negro boy really died. "Wisteria is a clinging vine," he writes today. "It

7 Owen Wister observed: "The more restless they are, the louder or more inarticulate is the singing, no words being used at all, but only a strange wailing. But as the cattle grow quiet, the music gathers form, and while the herd lies quietly at rest on the plain, the night herders are apt to sing long definite songs as they ride round and round the edges." (Journal entry, Texas, March 1893)

grows the way the old narratives do. But when I think of wisteria, it all comes back to me in fractals." The working novelist learns to respect cause and effect in his own way. One time, the old man was typing a passage about the hanging boy when his miner's headlight went out with no warning. (It's the ghost boy's doing. He must be growing stronger.) At once, his surroundings—the desk where he worked daily—became unfamiliar, a threatening trap. He was acutely aware of being underground. He ventured a few steps from his desk and was so disoriented he had to consciously take deep breaths before he started again. He took a long time to feel his way toward where he believed the ladder out should be. He struggled with the impossibility of contacting anyone on the surface. He felt swallowed up. Later, safe in his bed, he understood. The shelter had shown him its natural state; that is, when he introduced the headlight the real shelter had disappeared for a time and pretended to be a room for him. The technical cause: he'd opened the valve too far and let too much water onto the carbide—and blew out the lamp. The writer's reason: the shelter was the belly of the beast all along. The open coffin. Reading for Vincent's class, he would have skimmed a safe league above the glowing words of monstrous anglerfish "—all this to explain, would be to dive deeper than Ishmael can go. The subterranean miner that works in us all, how can one tell whither leads his shaft by the ever shifting, muffled sound of his pick?" decades before he needed them. Roe never specified the color, black or white, of his ghost boy.

"Origin of the Ghost Boy"

I circled back, ignoring the clothesline, just as my kid sister Penny banged the kitchen door and ran out into the yard calling for her damned cat. I got to the hatch just in time to avoid Penny but almost tripped over Tiger, who charged past and down into the shelter ahead of me. Every time her cat spied an open hatch, he came out of nowhere and impulsively threw himself down into the bunker, where, after he got his bearings, he flattened his whole body against the floor, believing himself to be safely and completely disappeared. I knew that was the reason cats get run over on the street. I could overhear bits of their talk through the air vent. I was committed to waiting it out right underneath their feet, until the last neighbor and family member and official of death finally cleared out, the last evidence and gossip gathered at the scene. A now hysterical Penny rattled the bushes looking for Tiger. I was afraid her cat's pitiful meows would turn their attention to the fallout shelter. I called to Tiger in a low familiar voice. Soon I felt the cat's whiskers on my hand before he licked it. I pet him, desperate to keep him calm, but it was hard work, all the adrenaline had tired me out. I didn't dare crank the pump to recirculate the heavy air. I dozed off. A noise woke me—I can only liken it these years later to the sound of two saints locked in combat, their boots slipping in vomit as they fought over me—Tiger's back arched beneath my hand, his thick tail madly twitching against my leg. His whole body was vibrating from within. The cat and I heard the wings' brief beat against the low ceiling followed by the drop to our feet of something sentient.[8] A fucking bird, down here? Tiger was instantly upon the thing out in the blackness. The winged one fluttered, chirping rapidly in a hopping flight, then became all screeches. I recognized the sounds, unmistakable, having killed one in my bedroom. Tiger was attacking a bat! The chamber had no corners for hiding, and both cat and bat were able to maneuver in the dark—I feared I'd get in between them without knowing it until it was too late. Bats might be rabid: one scratch and I'd be in trouble. It revolted me to imagine the bat flying at my face. All this commotion was sure to betray me at any moment and they would come looking for me down here. A bat squeak, the thud against the thick wall, then nothing more. I exhaled. Tiger must have broken the creature's neck.

We ran like murderers in all directions, as if on cue, not one of us daring to witness whatever was about to come and be punished for it. We took off in all directions then met at the ball field, which drew us like a magnet even this afternoon. I remember I was the last boy to straggle in—I'd been hiding beside the creek—they were already cooking up our alibi: we'd played baseball all day, just like every day—and I too swore an oath to stick to one story or kill the bastard who broke down. "If they press you for details, give them the lowdown on yesterday's game." Before suppertime, the state troopers went door to door up our block and interrogated each child and interviewed the parents separately. I grew insanely

8 "Presently I became aware of a singular hissing sound close at my ears, and discovered it to proceed from Tiger, who was panting and wheezing in a state of the greatest apparent excitement, his eyeballs flashing fiercely through the gloom..." (*Pym*)

nervous counting down the houses to mine. I had never before that hour felt the terrible passage of time.

Penny testified: "I thought it was a dummy hanging there from the clothesline. Not Gerald. I thought it was a joke because it looked smaller than a person. I was looking for my kitty and the sheets on the clothesline kept drifting in the wind so I couldn't clearly see. Then I realized there had been an accident and I couldn't stop screaming and ran back to the house." I testified: "He had no reason that I know of for taking his own life like that. An unlikely candidate, I'd say. He was such a happy kid. The boys on the street took him in, treated him like everybody's little brother. He was going to the movies later, his favorite thing in the world." The term hate crime had yet to be coined. The tall trooper looped the chin strap of his wide-brim hat over the handle as he listened. The revolver in his holster looked enormous.

Then at bedtime, Mom and Dad sat on my bed, weighing down both sides of the mattress, spoon feeding me more questions with matching answers. Dad had convinced himself. "I didn't like the looks of that young cop, did you see him? I know his daddy. Gets paid big bucks to walk around the factory all night with a broom, never worked a day in his life and thinks he's smarter than the rest of us who work for a living. His patrolman kid will look just like the old man in 20 years. Got in some trouble at the high school running cars drunk." My mother kissed me on my forehead for the first time in years: "Say a special prayer for Gerald tonight, buddy." She knew I didn't pray any more.

The town's one-man police force had to be called away

from his full-time job at the dry-cleaners. Officer Perry responded to a 2:43 pm call about a child not breathing in the 100 block of Liberty Street. He arrived on the scene just as the state patrol cruiser pulled in. A little guy with a crumpled hat was already busy snapping photographs all around the place and not touching anything. The victim was driven to Doctor Richard Avery's office, one block away, where he was pronounced DOA at 2:51 pm. While the state police troopers were building a victimology from friends, family, neighbors detailing the boy's likes and dislikes, hobbies, sexuality, any history of drug or alcohol use, Officer Perry told the *Chronicle* reporter that 12-year-old Gerald Swyers, a well-liked elementary school student and the only son of the Akron basketball player Leroy Swyers, had been playing alone in the backyard of his parents' home when he accidentally hanged himself with a makeshift lasso he'd fashioned from clothesline. No foul play was suspected. He went on to speculate that the Negro boy may have been imitating a stunt he'd seen in a cowboy movie. The Ohio State Highway Patrol and the Medina County Department of Child Welfare are investigating pending the coroner's report, he said. Authorities have successfully located and interviewed the neighbors, friends, and family of the deceased. No suicide note was found. How to describe the death to a readership who believed it possible that a munchkin hanging himself out of unrequited love for a munchkin actress is caught on camera at the very end of the Tin Woodsman discovery scene? From the autopsy report: "...complete suspension of the body...ligature material was the plastic rope found around the neck...an oblique-shaped ligature mark showing black friction burn of the skin...cervical vertebra was found intact...damage to neck muscle fibers and hemorrhage at the Sternal end of the Sternocleido-mastoid muscle...also present...thyroid cartilage found intact; no damage to hyoid bone...." At length, the coroner's office ruled the local Negro boy, age 11 years and nine months, died by suicide. The neck was not broken, and an overturned galvanized bucket was found close to the body. The coroner surmised that the boy had stood tip toes on top of the bucket until he decided to kick it away. Considering that the end would have taken from 20 to 30 minutes, the victim must have planned the act for a time when he was not likely to be discovered for half an hour. Word around town was the Swyers boy died accidentally, the tragic victim of play gone terribly wrong. The boy was alone in his backyard when he attempted to reenact the frontier hangings in his favorite cowboy movies. This account soon passed into small town legend and bed-time admonitions from parents about television and movies and letting your imagination go wild. Of course, we knew it was murder. The last people to see Gerald alive conspired to tell one lie and stick by it for life. We didn't say he panicked when he slipped off the bucket and only made things worse by pulling on the noose with both hands. We didn't say no one tried to hold him up or cut him down. That if we saved him there'd be hell to pay. That it was either him or us so it had to be him. It came easy to say we'd been playing baseball until no one asked us to say it again.

As it turned out, nothing could be avoided, nothing was easy. The boys were dressed up and called upon to act their parts in the screenplay version of Gerald's death. The day of Gerald's funeral, my whole school was dismissed and we were herded across the street into the white Methodist church and marched single file past his open coffin. Gerald was wearing his Lash LaRue neckerchief in there. His parents arranged for him to wear it, concealing the wound to his neck. I didn't look at his face above the black neckerchief. Mom said he looked like a porcelain doll, the mortician had to use so much makeup, but I picture Emmett Till's tortured face. The trick I'd learned at funerals for grandparents was not to look directly into their wax faces. Strictly avoid getting stuck on that final image whenever you remember them. All I clearly remember is his neckerchief and my knife and the overwhelming odor of wisteria. Nobody seemed to notice when I dropped my Lash and Black Diamond penknife inside the padded coffin. He was buried in some little town in another county and his parents soon moved there. Our town returned to being all white for another generation.

**Notes from the Blue Notebook**

Lash LaRue westerns are country club Caucasian. A single Indian has a speaking part in the whole series, and the effect is comedic closure, bringing down the curtain on one film with a laugh. "Piute," a stone-faced no-speakum Injun played by Frank Lackteen in *Son of a Badman*, bowls over Fuzzy by replying in a perfect Oxford accent.[9]

9 Steve Adams, hero of the popular "Straight Arrow" radio program, newspaper strip, and comic book series, transformed from "white" rancher into an avenging Comanche warrior to combat bad guys and natural disasters. His secret was that he was born a Comanche.

Akron native Jim Jarmusch's Indian named Nobody is a reader of William Blake and Johnny Depp plays a Cleveland, Ohio accountant cum accidental western hero, *Dead Man* in effect bringing down the curtain on the formula western film in 1995.

In 2018, after decades of resisting desegregation the Akron Baptist Temple and its 30-acre campus sold to The Word Church, joining its predominantly black congregations in Warrensville, Cleveland, as well as Akron, for $1.5 million.

**"Imaginary Form Rejection"**

Thank You for Letting Us Read Your Manuscript.

This book demonstrates no real understanding of narrative development, nor does it appear to be an experiment in fiction or, for that matter, how to manage a paragraph. Its setting seems drawn with a favorite crayon. The reader cannot picture the characters; the narrator remains there but invisible like wallpaper. The author is apparently uninterested in dialog or how a person might address another person and be fathomed. This book is untouched by psychology. I cannot call to mind a single thing I have read in a hundred pages. Let me suggest that the theme of this book is bad writing. Too short to be called a novel.

—The Editors.

**"What Happened to the Old Gang"**

I learned, from his obituary, that Clifford Eugene Dollar was a lifetime resident of Guilford Township, Medina County. At the time of his death, he was employed as a security guard for the Blue Tip Match Company in Wadsworth. "Cliff" was a Civil War reenactment enthusiast and also enjoyed hunting and taxidermy. Jimmy (Jar) Jarmusch was a natural athlete, short and stocky, who played all sports in high school. His family house was painted lime green in the fashion of his parents' heritage. His father, a janitor in a factory, suffered severe depression and could always be found sitting silently beside the kitchen stove warming himself. The night Jar and I egged cars from the cemetery across the street from his house, then jumped if the headlights turned onto the cemetery trees into an open grave they'd dug. After college, he went to work as an accountant for Hoover in North Canton; transferred to Aurora, Colorado, where he and his wife have lived since 1980. The only Catholic in the gang. Gary Ikles, compulsive collector of baseball gum cards and high school mathematical genius, died in a Jeep accident in Korea. Danny Tyler succeeded his father in the family's long-distance trucking business. Three-term mayor of the hometown. Past president of the town historical society. Never known to read a book in high school. Gil Carter, in spite of his short stature, starred as the high school quarterback and scoring guard on the basketball teams. After playing college baseball at the University of Arizona, he returned to his hometown to begin his fabled coaching career. As basketball coach, he holds the consolidated school's all-time record for victories. He plays golf with a handicap. Don Martin is what is meant by the old term Ohio Republican. Farmed his family's 300 acres then lived on in the homestead, just beyond the city limits, after his father's death at a good age. His heifers have won many ribbons at the county fair over the years.

Became a volunteer firefighter and, like his grandfather, made chief. Married his childhood sweetheart, who owns a chiropractic clinic and sews quilts.*

*Unattributed attributes: No relation to the film-maker...A school bus driver for the district for 34 years... Taught himself to play electric bass and enjoyed performing weekends in various bands over the years...Earned his private pilot's license...Mildly claustrophobic...Deathly afraid of big dogs...Wore the same haircut since eighth grade...Avid collector of post cards...Past operator of a bed-n-breakfast on High Street...After losing a leg to diabetes...Over the years grew suspicious of bird watchers... Never entered an art museum...He and his bride were called to be overseas missionaries...A single car followed his hearse to the cemetery...Acute visual and mental tunnel vision...Mildly hard of hearing in crowds but never missed a meeting of...One-eighth Cherokee...Nauseated by the smell of butterscotch ever since...The time his family left him in a truck stop restroom and didn't miss him until they'd already driven 40 miles...Color blind...His hair turned completely grey in high school...Crowd-scene extra in *Slap Shot*...Ate a peanut butter sandwich every day for over 65 years...Allergic to nuts...Built and flew his own airplane...Does not appear in the U.S. Census after 1980...Some will remember him as that crazy guy who stood on the corner of Liberty Street and gave away money...Enjoyed cutting wood...Enjoyed conversation before the trucking accident...Especially enjoyed walleye fishing and woodworking...Afraid to go near water.

**"What Happened to the Artist"**

The artist's last view of the earth was from a small plane, the land was a beautiful idea and the artificial horizon on the control panel was especially beautiful, then the reality of the earth without ideas rushing up to meet him. Nancy Holt oversaw the completion of "Amarillo Ramp," the open ogee of piled rock, having already outlasted its artificial lake, is gradually eroding.

After the shootings, someone painted "May 4, Kent 70" in white on the lintel, this graffiti was topical at the moment but can be seen to be antithetical to Smithson's theme of entropy, before long the white pigment was absorbed into the rough wood and faded in the weather, or maybe Smithson got his museum without walls and windows (frames) after all. On January 7, 1970 (unrelated to Robert Duncan's 51st birthday), he supervised 20 dump truck loads of dirt onto the roof of the nondescript abandoned outbuilding, the load cracking the central beam as planned, although Smithson had originally envisioned for a mud pour on the site but the weather was freezing. The visiting artist donated "Partially Buried Wood Shed, Kent State" to the university after professors valued the work at $10,000, an arsonist on March 28, 1975 destroyed a side of the construct, next month the university screened off the site with a grove of trees, on May 3, 1975 Nancy Holt who was Smithson's widow visited Kent State and called for the university to preserve the site already being catalogued among Smithson's important works, a university committee recommends demolition of the site but President Glenn Olds tables the recommendation in 1976, the shed's central beam fully breaks in 1981, in January 1984 the university removes all remaining traces of the work of art while artists and scholars continue to visit the unmarked site. In 2016, the university places a historical marker at the site ("...began January 7, 1970.").

**"Buried Architecture"**

"At Vestmann Islands an entire community was submerged in black ashes. It created a kind of buried house system...You might say that provided a temporary kind of buried architecture which reminds me of my own *Partially Buried Woodshed* out in Kent State, Ohio...one of the local papers...didn't really see that as a very positive gesture, and there was a rather disparaging article that went under the heading 'It's a Mud Mud Mud World.'"

Compass doesn't work down there. Even more befuddling for a writer in the 20th century is the complete absence of a horizon—even Jackson Pollock had that endless distance of horizon to paint. The poet tod thilleman wondered aloud, upon surfacing from reading in *Artforum International* Thomas McEvilley's article "Art in the Dark," whether the ordeal in a fallout shelter without heat or electricity might qualify the old man as some kind of a performance artist.

**"They Turn Up the House Lights"**

Twice a year, between features the previously faceless theater manager appeared on stage as himself to innocent hisses and boos and, dutifully ignoring a paper airplane launched from the balcony rabble, raffled off a live turkey for Thanksgiving and a pet rabbit at Eastertime. The man expertly gripped the hapless gobbler upside down by its legs in one hand; the gaudy hare seemed to exhibit disabling stage fright. I was relieved when I didn't win a bird on domestic death row, and I vowed Mom and I would wash the pink dye from the nervous bunny's fur if only I could take him home.

**[Timeline for Lash LaRue]**

E.C. Roe compiled a Timeline, reproduced below, to address continuity during the writing of "Preacher." The most essential facts of Lash LaRue's life and careers remain obscure. It is no wonder that one of LaRue's favorite movies was *Outlaw Country*, in which he played the roles of Lash and his twin brother, The Frontier Phantom.

1. Above all, the Lash we watch in the movies is a Hollywood Apollo battling the renegade Dionysus *inside himself* to a draw.

2. Birth name and place of birth for LaRue remain in dispute. Books and magazines routinely claim Alfred Wilson LaRue was born in Gretna, Louisiana, but also in various towns in Michigan, Ohio, and Texas. Recent research of birth records online indicates our man is Rey Alfred Wilson, born on June 15, 1917, in Watervliet, Michigan.

3. Lash LaRue appears in *Wild West*, his second western and also his second Eddie Dean movie, in 1946, the year of the Nuremberg executions.

4. Fawcett reported 12 million copies of *Lash LaRue Western* comic books sold in 1952 alone. Cover photos for numbers 43 through 46 show Lash in vest and tie, about how he looked at fairs and personal appearances in the 50s.

5. Lash LaRue drew big crowds full of women and children at theaters and fairs from Texas to the Carolinas in the early 1950s. Lash didn't travel with Fuzzy, although fans swore a bearded comic dressed like him was St. John in the flesh.

6. In 1953, LaRue was involved in the widely reported "Memphis Sewing Machine Caper." He was arrested by Memphis police for possession of stolen goods, and again for receiving stolen goods. A Lash LaRue employee had bought up hot sewing machines to resell for profit. The MPD confiscated LaRue's pistol.

7. Newspaper headline, from 1956: "Lash LaRue Seized." Arrested a second time in Memphis for fencing hot property, LaRue said, "I bought an adding machine that happened to be stolen."

8. Guest stars in 17 episodes of Hugh O'Brien's *The Life and Legend of Wyatt Earp* television show, from 1956-57 and 1959-1960. LaRue could also be seen regularly on TV during this period on *Judge Roy Bean* and *26 Men.*

9. The low-budget feature film *Guns Don't Argue,* assembled from three episodes of the 1952 TV series *Gangbusters,* is released in 1957 among the pro-FBI propaganda emergent from those left working in Hollywood who were not black-balled. LaRue plays the doomed Doc Barker to Jean Harvey's Tommy-gun-wielding Ma Barker, reminding some that LaRue once had been cast as shotgun-toting Sarah Padden's doomed long-lost son. The historical Doc, the most pathologically violent Barker Gang member, was shot to death in the 30s in San Francisco Bay after escaping from Alcatraz. In the film, Lash is relaxing on his bed, reading a letter from Ma, when two G Men bust in and arrest him. He is outfitted in pleated slacks and open shirt, the picture of a good boy in the 50s.

10. Al LaRue married at least 11 times (some were bigamous liaisons), three times in the 1950s. He met Barbara Fuller, wife number three, at a Texas fair between filming. Reno Brown, his fourth wife, was born in Reno, Nevada, where she and LaRue kept a bar and motel. During the Reno years, he was breaking into TV. Paddie LaRue was his fifth wife and mother of his two sons. Al LaRue started drinking dangerously in the aftermath of his breakup with Paddie (the divorce is finalized in 1958). Oddly, the Lash LaRue character wins the girl in only a single film, *Law of the Lash.*

11. Around the end of his marriage with Reno Brown, LaRue attended a Rev. Bob Woodward sermon and was saved. (Reno says she didn't want to be married to a religious fanatic.) At first, Woodward had supported himself by spreading God's word at small churches and taking free will offerings. By 1980, he established the non-profit F.G.S. Productions.

12. A Bob Woodward (no relation) was a stuntman for Lash LaRue films.

13. Sometime after his divorce from Reno Brown, Lash LaRue was busted for possession of marijuana in Mt. View, Georgia. In his defense, LaRue told the judge he'd traded a Bible with a drug dealer for the dope, in hopes of saving the man from a life of drugs, and hadn't had time to properly dispose of it before he was apprehended.

14. The last *Lash LaRue Western* comic book (number 84) was printed in June 1961, the month Ernie Banks ended his 717 consecutive games-played streak.

15. In the 60s, you might catch "Lucky LaRue" playing R and B guitar in jam sessions at New Orleans' Dew Drop Inn.

16. The *New York Times* for January 7, 1966 prints the notice of Lash LaRue's arrest for vagrancy

among big ads for new movies *The Magnificent Men in their Flying Machines* and *Darling*. Police reported finding 35 cents in his pockets.

17. Lash LaRue made the cover of the magazine for Rev. James E. Ewing's Church of the Home, *World Compassion*, for July 1968. Six pages inside is "Western Movie Star Gets Saved and Filled with the Holy Ghost," a collage of film stills and a contemporary portrait of LaRue. Rev. Ewing, a former tent revival preacher, operated a direct-mail empire from his mansion in LA. The faithful were directed to send letters containing prayer requests and faith offerings to a post office box in Tulsa.

18. Lash LaRue is baptized by total immersion for a second time by Dr. Jimmy G. Tharpe at the Shreveport Baptist Tabernacle. "Brother Jimmy" was the founder of Baptist Christian College and Louisiana Baptist University, both unaccredited schools, as well as some 75 churches in Louisiana.

19. For a time, LaRue lived on free will collections from church-goers. Calling himself "Dr. LaRue," he became associated with John Cook, a/k/a "John 3:16," a self-styled evangelist and colporteur in Florida. LaRue would warm up the crowd with a brief personal-life "witness" before Cook's sermons.[10] (See reports of various legal problems with

10 Apparently, the effect was something like *Mexico City Blues* meets *Wise Blood*.

the Cook mission in St. Petersburg and Jacksonville newspapers.)

20. Later claiming he'd been unaware the film he was making was porn, LaRue plays Slade in Greg Corarito's *Hard on the Trail* (1971). Slade is an old guy (grey beard, very black eyebrows, a hat and vest) remarkable only for the fact that he was once The Lash LaRue. In one scene, Slade instructs some young bucks in the art of the whip.

21. Starting with the 1972 show at the Peabody Hotel in Memphis, with guest star Lash LaRue, the mid-70s saw the advent of the big western film festival, most notably in Nashville, Tampa, and St. Louis. LaRue worked the shows and also contracted for jobs with people he met at shows. He became a traveling celebrity for hire by church groups, hospitals, fairs, and sales groups. LaRue did PR for a chain of trailer sales dealerships in Arkansas and Texas—he showed up, popped the whip, and signed autographs. The Francis Tarkenton Agency paid LaRue $1,500 to attend a doctor's birthday party. Lash LaRue could sign his autograph in return for work on his car.

22. The cursive L's in his signature loop tiny black whips surrounding the corporeal "ash."

23. Becomes one of the first recipients, in 1983, of the Golden Boots Award.

24. "The sound is the breaking of the sound barrier," Lash explains during his demonstration of how to crack a whip on *The David Letterman Show* on February 16, 1984. The segment opened with the bullwhip showdown from *King of the Bullwhip.* The appearance ended with LaRue shredding newspaper and paper targets held out by a game but amusingly reluctant Letterman. "The end of the whip is like your arm," Lash advises Dave, as he wraps his whip around the host's arm to the delight of the studio audience.

25. Lash LaRue is widely credited with teaching Harrison Ford how to handle a bullwhip for *The Temple of Doom* (1984), as if to establish the first Indiana Jones movie in a tradition of action serials. For subsequent films in the series, Irish stuntman Bronco McLoughlin and Anthony DeLongis were hired as Ford's bullwhip tutor. Indiana Jones in all the films uses Australian bullwhips made by David Morgan from braided kangaroo hide.

26. Phil Smoot directed two B-films in 1985, both featuring Lash LaRue. A band of beautiful cowgirls enlist the help of Sheriff LaRue in *Alien Outlaw* to keep horse-riding Colt-shooting aliens, whose flying saucer has crashed in the North Carolina desert (sic.), from enslaving humans. In *The Dark Power,* exorcist LaRue is called in by a couple whose house, built over a cemetery, is haunted by Toltec zombies who awake hungry every thousand years.

27. From "Hoist 'Em, Pards, Lash Is Back," *People*, April 1, 1985, a feature story in advance of the release of *The Dark Power*:

a. "Lash LaRue ducks questions about his past like an old gunfighter dodging bullets. Ask about his marriages (nine, I've been told) or his run-ins with law, and he clouds over and answers with a line from an old Lord Buckley routine—stock footage that he's obviously unreeled before."

b. There was his guest role on the *Wyatt Earp* TV series. Arrested in 1956 for fencing stolen property. LaRue's Great Western Show toured the United States and Canada. Then, in the 60s, he bought a Nevada motel with his wife Reno Brown. He was saved again and began speaking before church groups—she divorced him for being a religious fanatic. The Florida arrest for vagrancy. The Georgia arrest for possession of marijuana; beat on appeal. Living on love offerings, speaking several times a week sponsored by Rev. Tom Popelka, then with evangelist John Cook.

c. "I'm a witness of a sort. I spent 40 years in the wilderness before God opened my spiritual eyes. As soon as I have the attention that's worthy of that which will yet be said, I'll speak authoritatively of one who has been and is not evidently dead. But I'm not fooling myself; I could never be righteous. As I study it, none are."

d. Describes LaRue's "eclectic blend of beliefs—old-time fundamentalism, Eastern mysticism and reincarnation."

e. Left the ministry to become a celebrity for hire, showing up at personal appearances for car dealerships, a mobile home distributor, a clothing manufacturer. "I just go where I feel. I'm not raisin' a garden."

f. Denied a pension by the Screen Actors Guild because much of his work was nonunion.

28. Sometime around 1986, the Christian Broadcasting Network purchased all the Lash LaRue films. (Find out why?)

29. Lash LaRue appears on the cover for the LP *Heroes* (Columbia, 1986), on the front cover with his whip, and on the back with Johnny Cash and Waylon Jennings. In 1948, 10-year-old Waylon went to see Lash LaRue at his local theater in Littlefield, Texas. The boy was among kids picked to come up on stage and hold targets for the whip act. Frightened, he screamed and wet his pants. By age 12, Waylon Jennings regularly performed over KVOW radio.

30. Also in 1986, LaRue played a minor character in the Jennings and Cash made-for-TV redo of the western film classic *Stagecoach*, joining Willie Nel-

son and Kris Kristofferson, the rest of supergroup The Highwaymen. Four years later, LaRue evanesced in his final film, *Pair of Aces*, another Nelson and Kristofferson TV vehicle.

31. "Nobody would have ever picked me to carry a message, but He did. I think we've been caught up in a circle of distortion and destruction"—LaRue interview in Raleigh, North Carolina newspaper *The Cary News*, January 28, 1987.

32. Charles Sharpe tells a story from the July 1989 Raleigh festival. That Saturday morning, Lash and the Sharpes meet for breakfast across the street from the venue. When Sharpe's wife complains it's too warm in the restaurant, the waitress responds, Oh, that ceiling fan hasn't worked in years. Lash looks around the table of sweltering people then quietly addresses the motionless fan: "Lord, it sure is warm down here, and we could use a bit of air." That fan begins to turn and soon it cools down their table. Lash says, "Thank you, Lord," and then, to the astonished waitress, "I believe we are ready to order now." (Charles M. Sharpe, *Lash LaRue, the King of the Bullwhip: The Man not the Legend*, 1996)

33. *Entertainment Tonight* aired the Garret Glaser interview with Lash LaRue from an Atlanta memorabilia show from the late 80s. The bullwhip duel from *King of the Bullwhip* opens the segment showing footage of Lash artfully popping his whip

and graciously signing autographs. Lash talks easily to Glaser while sensational still images of old newspaper clippings flash by: "'LaRue Saved From Sleep Pills, Jailed: Traffic Ticket Jugs Film Cowboy'"—"Long Beach jail…rushed to hospital when police found him unresponsive at 1857 Lime Ave., when they were serving a warrant for his arrest after he failed to appear in court for speeding ticket."…"Lash LaRue Seized; Girl Tries Suicide"—-Memphis, September 28…"Lash LaRue Held With 2 in Theft"—fencing stolen property, Memphis! Garret Glaser was himself a story when he became the first gay U.S. journalist to "come out." His landmark declaration came in a speech before executives at the 1992 convention of the Radio/TV Directors Association, in San Antonio.

34. A reporter for the Charlotte *Observer* published a scathing review of his boyhood hero Lash LaRue's behavior at the July 1991 film festival. By the 1990s, Charles Sharpe sat next to LaRue's side so he could repeat into his good ear what the fan wanted to be inscribed.

35. Printed on the back of a promotional card photograph showing Lash in full costume and armed with gun and whip is a poem "Conscienced [sic.] and written by Lash LaRue." The poem of 8 stanzas ends, a dozen stolen flowers for his urn:

*I know some day*
*We all will see*
*A world at peace*
*In tranquility*

*When men shall find*
*The time again*
*To voice a praise to God and*
*Then*
*Man's right to Life and Liberty*
*would never cease*
*And the world will find*
*An Everlasting Peace.*

36. His cremated ashes were held at Forest Lawn during a lengthy family dispute before being laid to rest in a vault in Calverton National Cemetery, Suffolk County, New York, the largest and busiest U.S. national cemetery. Calverton, New York is home to the Naval Weapons Industrial Reserve Plant, a test facility for jet fighters.

37. Among the actor's papers was found his copy of *The Virginian*, with its 50-dollar bill bookmark still crisp inside.

**"Biographical Sketch of the Author"**

O stint not your applause, for he is that star-faced clown who jumped from a considerable height into a tumbler of ordinary water for you.

O, retail not your affection, for he contains that multitude of starry-eyed clowns emergent from a tiny car. For your amusement and edification, ladies and gents, the water glass is the old man's trick bunker with a false bottom; around him all the characters in his story spring improbably from his idling quarantined brain.

**"More Advanced Praise for 'Preacher'"**

"To keep his throat elevated<br>
the old man has to sleep in a chair,<br>
the only patron in the house<br>
before the movie dawns."

—AGUSTÍN FERNÁNDEZ MALLO,<br>
author of *The Nocilla Trilogy*.

**"Additional Dialog by Mr. LaRue"**

(Some godforsaken motel off the convention center)

Getting so it takes a shot to get a man to rise from bed by noon.

High bleeping noon, alright.

Harder and harder way to eke out a living, in drips and drabs, seems the only way I can make it is to disappear-from the signing tables every chance I get, when the line thins out, have me a nip from the bottle in the get-away car.

You name it I sign anything, or sell them a glossy photograph with my verse on the reverse and sign that,

*To My Friend, Ricky.*

From Texas to Carolina, the ladies still admire the way I address them.

The ladies know I love them all.

This is a three-"Where's Fuzzy? I just love Fuzzy to death."-per-hour crowd.

(Al succumbed 25 years ago from long-term alcohol abuse or spousal abuse.)

Sign,

pop the whip.

Then I mount Black Diamond, let him rear up twice, and ride out of town.

What's this town, this morning?

(Proposed copy for "Preacher" dustcover)

## 9. The Virginian

To this day, the Owen Wister Award is presented annually by the Western Writers of America for lifetime achievement in the field of the western. The old man's correspondent Will Henry was the first recipient of the award in 1960. Known as the Saddleman Award, it originally honored the best western book of the year; in recent years, award winners have included John Wayne and Clint Eastwood.

Los Angeles wildfires, driven by strong winds and stoked by climate change, prompted energy suppliers to cut off power throughout the region: the Getty Fire threatened the Getty Museum, and the Easy Fire encroached on the Ronald Reagan Presidential Library, the old man pauses before continuing to type, where the former president and first lady are buried, and forced the evacuation of hundreds of thousands of people from their homes.

"No more," the White House responded, threatening to cut off federal funds to fight California wildfires. President Trump tweeted Gavin Newsom that the Democratic governor of a blue state that went to Hillary Clinton by 61.7% in 2016 needs to "get his act together" and manage the cleaning of combustible debris from his state's forest floors. Federal agencies own and oversee 19 million of California's 33 million forested acres.

The Sylmar brush fire, in October, reached the Iverson Ranch, half a century after the Chatsworth-Malibu Fire swept through the iconic site for countless western films, destroying all man-made structures.

# 10. Preacher

**"Firey Sunsets, Black and White"**

The victims in the California movie house fire were trampled underfoot in the stampede for the only exit, reported the fire marshal following a lengthy investigation. (Newspaper clipping)

The horses have been pushed too far in this sun. They are lathered, shivering beneath the heavy, ornate saddles, suffering while their lungs burn all the oxygen. The director is ordering yet another gallop past the cameras. Look smart, now—before we lose the light! But all the riders have floated off like smoke.

Goethe as an old man called the fifth act of *Faust, Part II*, "Open Country" (*"Offene Gegend"*).

**Early Draft, Opening to "Preacher"**

THE BOY IN THE BLACK felt Stetson hadn't closed his blue eyes all night and ate no breakfast, so he and his father were among the first in line outside the Norka. The boy stomping in his stiff new cowboy boots and breathing plumes into the unwarmed morning air. The father, always nervous to be in the city, lighting one Camel on another but without complaint. The boy could hardly keep from bolting into the street each time a likely sedan slowed up. For this day was the day Lash LaRue was coming to Akron!

On rare occasions on their rare trips into the city,

more paternal whim than a reward for the boy, his father would treat him to a plain hamburger and grape Nehi at the Atomic Grill, a converted railroad car dry-docked in an alley a block behind the theater. That made the day. More often, the father was in a depressed mood or there wasn't the money that week. Or it never occurred to the father. And the boy knew he could never lobby to eat at the Atomic—that would break the magic spell and, poof, the diner would return to the tracks.

This part of the city always evoked a memory from the boy's early childhood. Or, to say it more accurately, he remembered being told that he was taken downtown to see Admiral Byrd. "The explorer had a vehicle made for five million dollars, called The Snow Cruiser, and he visited Akron to have special tires put on it at Goodyear. I don't remember actually seeing Admiral Byrd but I was told the anecdote so many times by Uncle Booth it makes a memory. "Admiral Byrd took The Snow Cruiser to the Antarctic in 1940. The machine was 55 feet long, 12 feet high, and 15 feet wide. The tires that occasioned his visit to Akron were 10 feet in diameter and three feet in width. The reason for the vehicle's length and the size of its tires probably was to enable it to traverse a crevasse and not get hung up.

"I was told that Admiral Byrd left The Snow Cruiser parked on the ice when he left the Antarctic and came back to the U.S. The ice floe he left it on broke away from the main ice sheet and drifted out to sea. The Cruiser is now at the bottom of the ocean...."

It began to spit snow. Snowflakes on the navy blue sleeve of his father's pea coat did not melt.

"This is the best day of my life," the boy told himself and not his father.

(End of the second reel.)

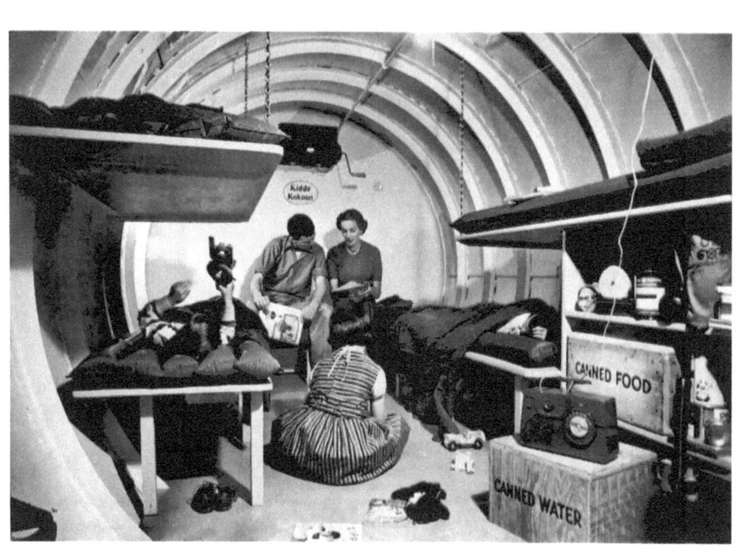
Kidde Kokoon
CANNED FOOD
CANNED WATER

10333
NORMAL
GROUND
LEVEL

www.ingramcontent.com/pod-product-compliance
Lightning Source LLC
Chambersburg PA
CBHW020332310726
48979CB00015B/2341/J

* 9 7 8 1 9 5 2 4 1 9 2 7 0 *